Fishing for Chickens

SELECTED PERSEA ANTHOLOGIES

Fishing for Chickens

SHORT STORIES ABOUT RURAL YOUTH

Edited, with an introduction by Jim Heynen

A Karen and Michael Braziller Book
PERSEA BOOKS / NEW YORK

Acknowledgments

Thanks to many people for their advice and suggestions, including David Bengston, Robert Hedin, Jonis Agee, Kim Stafford, Scott Sanders, John Zdrazil, Naomi Shihab Nye, Bill Ransom, Jan Marts, James R. Hepworth, James Schaap, Bill Holm, David Pichaske, Jim Bodeen, Patrick Parks, Tree Swenson, Danny Rendleman, Jan Worth, Josip Novakovich, Dick Sowienski, John Rezmerski, Jan Allister, Mark Allister, Jane Yolen, Donald Hall, Tobias Wolff, Ron Hansen, Alvin Greenberg, Steve Sanfield, Jonathan Greene, Bill Kittredge, Wenda Clement, Paul Gruchow, Edie Clark, Erin Flanagan, Melanie Crow, Brian Bedard, Roy Parvin, Carroll Yoder, John Witte, Glen Love, Teresa Jordon, Rich Wandschneider, George Venn, Greg Booth, Karl Pohrt, Ellen Bass, Jonathan Greenberg, Rick Simonson, Terry Salvino, Don Lee, and especially the people at Persea Books: Karen Braziller and Gayle Greeno.   —J.H.

The publisher wishes to thank Roberta Garris, who expressed a need for a book that reflected her students' lives and provided the inspiration for this anthology.

For information, write to the publisher:
Persea Books, Inc.
171 Madison Avenue
New York, New York 10016

Library of Congress Cataloging-in-Publication Data

Fishing for chickens : short stories about rural youth / edited, with an introduction by Jim Heynen.
        p. cm.
     "A Karen and Michael Braziller book."
     ISBN 0-89255-264-6 (alk. paper) — ISBN 0-89255-265-4 (pbk. : alk. paper)
     1. Rural youth—Fiction. 2. United States—Social life and customs—20th
century—Fiction. 3. Short stories, American. I. Heynen, Jim, 1940–

PS648.R85 F57 2001
813'.0108321734—dc21   2001021494

Designed by Rita Lascaro. Set in Stone Serif and Swing.
Manufactured in the United States of America.
FIRST EDITION

Contents

Introduction

I met a well-dressed lawyer recently who said he grew up on a farm in Kentucky. "Is that so?" I said. "Let me see your scars."

He held out his left palm. The jagged scar told me he'd once had a bad cut that healed without stitches. "I got this from grabbing a barbed wire," he said, "and this scar on my chin is where a pony kicked me."

I grew up on a farm in northwest Iowa, in one of the last areas of the state to get electricity. I may not know everything about growing up rural, but I know rural folks have scars. This lawyer was the real thing.

Scars may be our badge of authenticity, but the differences go much deeper. It's true that, just like urban kids, we worried about doing well in school, we worried about who was and who wasn't our best friend, and we had spats with brothers and sisters and parents—but we still knew there were some basic differences. Most of us were poorer, or at least had far fewer conveniences. We probably spent more time with our families—usually helping them with the work that needed doing—and we also spent more time alone, often making friends with trees and meadows, or with animals—most of which were being raised for food.

Living close to nature and its creatures may be the most essential difference. In fact, for rural young people the land and its animals can be as much a part of daily life as family members. And like dealing with family members, dealing with the land and animals can bring both pleasure and pain. The weather can be treacherous, living conditions can be tough, and the work can often be exhausting and dangerous. Learning to love both wild and domestic animals requires openness to nature's wonders, as well as an awareness of pragmatic necessity. Rural kids often see the births and deaths of all kinds of creatures at a very early age. Sometimes they take in an orphaned lamb or chick and lovingly care for it, only to have to sacrifice it to dinner one day. They marvel at the beautiful pheasant or graceful deer glimpsed from afar, but they and their parents probably hunt for some of their food or know people who do. Chances are they've seen another pheasant or deer being brought home for a holiday meal. As common as these experiences are, it is still not easy for young people who can so easily identify with creatures who seem as vulnerable as they are themselves.

The stories included in this anthology are from all over the country and show young people in many different rural situations. From the hill country of the Northwest and South, to the breadbasket states of the Midwest, to the ranches and mountains and vegetable fields of the West, to the fishing waters off the coast of Alaska and pineapple canneries of Hawaii, to the frigid woods of the Northeast, the writers in this collection show young people both attached to the wonders of the natural world that rural living offers and yet coping with its peculiar challenges. What I find heartwarming is how openly the characters experience their various feelings.

Nature is not neutral for many of the characters. In Tony Earley's "Aliceville," the geese appear to the young boy "like a revelation" and make sounds as if speaking with "ancient tongues" before disappearing in the corn stubble "as if they had been ghosts." In Alma Villanueva's "Golden Glass," the fourteen-year-old Ted escapes the painful setting of a home in which his father is no longer present to find peace for the summer months in a fort he builds in the cypress trees. Often the natural world carries a sense of beauty and innocence that is in sharp contrast to the world of human behavior and experience. Vicky Wicks's "I Have the Serpent Brought" begins in an idyllic paradise where a young girl sits on her favorite rock recognizing and naming the various flowers. It is a world in which she can imagine making wild animals into pets or being carried blissfully away by a hawk before she is made to accept the adult perspective that sees the wild animals as a threat to the family's livelihood. In my own stories, "What Happened During the Ice Storm" and "Who Had Good Ears," "the boys" identify more with the wild birds than they do with the world of adults or the mechanized realities of a working farm.

The sharpest contrast between the world of humans and the world of nature occurs in Alice Walker's "The Flowers," a short tale about a ten-year-old-girl who enjoys the late-summer ripening crops (a setting which is to her a "golden surprise that caused little tremors to run up her jaws") before she wanders off to discover a human horror from the past.

Among the many stories in which animals have a central place, perhaps the most heartrending is Wallace Stegner's "The Colt." In this story, a colt is attacked by wild dogs through a boy's negligence and then becomes the object of the boy's total attention and affection. An animal is also a central character in Lewis Nordan's "Sugar Among the Chickens," but here the tone is largely comic as an eleven-year-old boy decides to fish for chickens on the farmyard because his mother won't let him walk to the town pond to fish.

"I have no time for track or basketball because I have too many chores," says the girl narrator in Nancy Brown's "Burn Pile." Although an animal has a central place in this story too (in this case, a baby vulture), this is one of several stories in which we see a young person having to accept the responsibilities of work—and the consequences of not meeting those responsibilities. As the father says in "Burn Pile," "you gotta have guts, skill, and smarts livin' in the country."

Work and the consequences of work weigh heavily in Jon Volkmer's "The Elevator Man." Not only do we see the twelve-year-old Tim struggling to measure up to his father's expectations of work in the grain elevator, but we also have the constant reminders of the damage that breathing milo dust can cause. Kathleen Tyau's "Pick Up Your Pine" is a grueling hard work story too, but this time it's in a Hawaiian pineapple cannery. A conspicuous image in this story is a red badge the narrator wears to indicate that she is a child laborer.

Because families or communities so often comprise a cooperative work unit in rural settings, not surprisingly family and human relationships are the central focus in several of the stories—though, even when this is true, the rural setting is still always a significant factor. Hisaye Yamamoto's "Seventeen Syllables" is a story rich in the complexities of family (a talented poet mother and a

jealous father) and friendship (the adolescent girl pro-
tagonist Rosie gets her first kiss from a Mexican boy
laborer), but the tomato fields hover throughout the
story, making their constant demands for picking and
packing. By the end of Rebecca Rule's "Walking the
Trapline," the chill of the landscape is reflected in the
father's chilly behavior toward his daughter and son,
but along the way the girl narrator appreciates the soft
fur of a female fisher her father has trapped by rubbing
it against her face. In Tomás Rivera's "The Salamanders"
the desperate migrant working family finds a dark unity
while dealing with the salamanders that invade their
tent. Eric Gansworth's "The Raleigh Man" tells the story
of a Native American boy who has to struggle with the
way members of his tribe lump the likable Raleigh Man
with other white people who are seen as threatening
reservation life. In Nora Dauenhauer's "Egg Boat," work
is more a matter of finding one's place in the family as
the Tlingit young girl sets out in her special little boat to
succeed in the summer troll-fishing expedition. In
Pinckney Benedict's "Miracle Boy," a farm accident has
made the Miracle Boy an easy victim for boyhood cru-
elty, but by the end he has become the hero in a story of
friendship and forgiveness.

I returned to my boyhood home in Northwest Iowa
recently, thinking about the stories in this collection. As
I rode with my brother through the countryside, he
pointed out what was happening. Fewer and fewer but
larger and larger farms. Huge feedlots. Fewer farm-
houses. And we both knew that the current census indi-
cated the same trend throughout the country. Many
farm workers in my boyhood community now live in

town and drive to the country to cultivate the crops and feed the animals. Agri-business is wiping out the rural experience as my brother and I knew it. I thought of Thomas Jefferson's fantasy of an America that would always largely be made up of hard-working rural people, and wondered if anything of that fantasy was being preserved. I wondered if we were coming to the end of an era in which people could write or tell stories about growing up rural.

Then we drove through my hometown. Six hundred Spanish-speaking people had moved to the area in recent years. "Where do they work?" I asked.

"The packing plant," he said. "Some work in dairies."

I thought of "The Elevator Man." I thought of "Pick Up Your Pine." I hoped that none of them would be telling stories that resembled "The Salamanders." I also thought of news stories I'd read of Cambodian and Ethiopian and Hmong people moving into the Midwest, many of them working in farm-related industries—field work, ethanol plants, turkey and bean-processing centers. I thought of "Seventeen Syllables."

Then we returned to the farm where I grew up. What had been the chicken coop when I was a boy is now a vacant building—or was a vacant building until recently when my grandnephew started a kind of fantasy animal project inside. He is raising beautiful pheasants, rabbits, exotic chickens. I thought of "Golden Glass." I thought of "I Have the Serpent Brought." I thought of my own bird-loving stories.

The final eye-opener of the weekend was noticing the badges of authenticity on my grandnephews' and grandnieces' skin. They are growing up rural. And they have scars. Good ones. It made me want to drive into town and visit the new Mexican restaurant. Maybe some of the people from the packing plant could tell me what my old rural community is like nowadays. Maybe we could compare scars. Maybe they could tell me a few stories that I could bend a little and make them my own. Maybe I could tell them a few that they could bend a little and make their own.

—Jim Heynen

Walking the Trapline

■ ■ ■

Rebecca Rule

My brother Thomas's snowshoes were bigger than mine, though he was smaller than me. Father made the snow-shoes. It took a long time because the ash for the frames had to be aged and steamed into shape. The deer hide had to be soaked in the brook until the hair floated off and then tanned in our cellar. One year the neighbor's dog dragged the hide out of the brook and chewed it. Father saw the tracks. He found the ruined hide. Later, he shot the dog. I think the neighbors knew, but they never said so.

On winter evenings, Father sliced the stiff hides into strips to soak in coffee cans till they were supple and slimy. He knotted them to the frames. His big, scarred hands squeaked each strand tight and even into place.

The small finger on Father's right hand was a shiny stub. The beaver trap had "snipped the little feller right off," he said, when he told the story. But I remembered the bloody mitten.

Father cut my leather harnesses plenty big for me to grow into. When the insides were webbed, dried, and varnished over, he sliced the harnesses thick and meas-ured them to my feet. As he knelt to adjust the buckles around my rubber boots, I saw his pale scalp through the thinning curls.

He was a young father just the same, with a hard jaw,

all his front teeth, and blue eyes that made me feel dirty when he stared at me. Mother said I had eyes like my father and asked what I was staring at all the time. She never asked him.

When I was eleven and Thomas was nine, Father began to teach him about the trapline. He allowed me to come along when the weather was fine and the dishes done.

Father trapped beaver through the ice, mink in the brooks, and fisher in the trees. He got good money for the pelts. He said his job at the tannery, which made him smell so sour, wouldn't be enough to feed us if it weren't for the animals he caught.

When Mother complained that he ought to be tending to the woodpile or the roof or the broken cellar steps, he'd say he trapped for the money and she should be glad. She'd stare him in the eye just a second till her face had to twitch away. She knew he trapped because he wanted to, and that was all.

He tended the sets he had to drive to in the evenings after work. On Sundays, he made the rounds of the traps in the big woods out behind our house.

"Do you think we'll catch anything today?" I asked, snowshoeing behind him and Thomas up the hill behind our house. The snow was new and light and clean. It barely held the imprint of my webbing.

"Your mother would rap me a good one if I came back with nothing, Elizabeth."

I laughed. She would never rap him, though she might get cross and not make supper if she thought he had wasted the whole day. When she did not make supper, Thomas and I went to our room early to get away from her silence.

I liked to step on the tails of Thomas's snowshoes and make him stumble when we walked downhill. Sometimes he'd stumble too far and jar Father. "Watch it, boy," Father would growl. And Thomas would look back at me real ugly.

"You see those tracks down over that banking?" Father stopped so quick I almost walked over Thomas.

"Yup," I replied.

"You see them swish marks and how square they are?"

"Yup," I replied. I could have told him what kind they were, but he always finished a lesson once he started it.

"A little female fisher," he said. "She's moving on a new snow. We might get up here a-ways and find her hanging in my little trap."

"I hope so," I said.

Father stared at Thomas until he looked up. "Wouldn't that be dandy, boy?"

Thomas nodded.

I curled my thumbs in my mittens. Mid-morning by the sun, and the air was still cold enough to stiffen the skin in my nose.

We found the trap empty and sprung. The bait was gone. Father picked up a feather. "Sprung by a Christly blue jay. Fisher came along, just climbed right up and ate that bait slick as a bean." He stomped the feathers into the snow. Thomas and I stood silent and close together, elbows rubbing. Better not make matters worse, we thought. Thomas and I thought about some things the same way. We'd catch one another's eye and understand that we were thinking and feeling the same.

"She'll be back," Father said.

"She'll be back," I said to Thomas, who knew as well

as I did that fisher travel in great circles and always come back.

Father pulled the pack basket off his back as if it wasn't heavy a bit. He laid it up against the leaning birch tree beside the ice chisel he carried like a staff. My father was strong. When the beaver trap sprung on one hand, he opened it with the other to free himself.

"Can we build a fire?" Thomas asked.

"What, you cold?"

"No." Thomas was shivering. I kicked him in the ankle, meaning "Tell him you're cold." Thomas knew what I meant, but clamped his mouth shut. He could be stubborn about things that didn't count.

"I'm cold," I said. It was all right for me to be cold.

Father didn't hear.

Thomas and I played tag to keep warm and threw snow at one another because we liked to. We were careful not to throw snow at Father. When he played snow fight, he'd run us down one at a time and rub our faces with snow.

"You kids get away from this set if you're going to raise hell," he said.

I sat by the pack, tired of the game anyhow. Thomas walked away.

"Reach in that bag and find my bottle of scent, Elizabeth." Father's scents were secret. He said they were made of deer glands, skunk juice, fish oil, and other secret things that no other trappers could know and we could never tell.

He had strung up the new piece of beaver carcass. He plucked a branch of hemlock and wired it over the meat—to make it look natural, he said. Fisher didn't know hemlock branches did not grow on birch trees.

Father didn't catch many fisher in a season; there weren't too many around. I had never seen one in a trap, only in the cellar when I watched the careful skinning and stretching. He had to peel the fur away from the flesh whole with his skinning knife, even to the tiny toes. Thomas wasn't allowed to skin. One rip ruined a good pelt. Father let Thomas skin our cat that died. Afterwards, Thomas whispered to me that skinning her had made him throw up in the bathroom, quiet so nobody would hear.

I glimpsed a fisher once. Father had said, "Look up, quick," and in the tree I'd seen the flash of darkness, the bouncing of the branch. "Fisher," he'd hissed, and the hiss made me tremble.

With a twig, Father dribbled the scent over the bait wired high as he could reach on the leaning tree. The scent was tangy as skunk and fresh as pine needles. One Halloween, he smeared it on the doorknob so when the neighbor's kids came begging, they'd get that smell on them to last a while. Father and I laughed and laughed to think of them eating their chocolate.

The steel-wire trap was nailed just below the bait. When set, it made a square for the animal to reach his head through. The trap would snap around the neck.

By the time we reached the farthest-out pond, the sun was gone, the day turned gray. Father left us the matches and told us to warm up while he made a set at the upper end of "the meadow." I called it a bog because of the ice, a beaver bog where dams had backed the water over part of the woods and the trees had died and silvered. Trunks stood straight and silent. Stumps tipped to the air and groped with twisted roots. All my nightmares occurred in beaver bogs. I told Thomas they were haunted.

Father saw the snow melted at the top of the beaver house. He knew the beaver were there, breathing. The single beaver he had left alive last year had formed a new colony. He never trapped all the beaver out of this pond because it was so handy to home: just five miles straight out the back door, a new colony almost every year.

Thomas and I watched him stride away up the bog. His tracks were wide apart and straight in a row. "I wish I hadn't come," Thomas mumbled.

"We're going to catch something pretty soon," I told him. But I knew he meant we had walked too far and the air was too cold. His black buckle boot had a barb-wire hole in it that let snow on his sock. His left foot had been frostbitten the winter before. He liked to complain about it.

"I don't care about this," said Thomas. He knew it might take Father hours to make the pole sets for the beaver. Then three miles to walk home; three and a half with the side trips we had to make for the other fisher traps. We wouldn't be home until dark.

We broke pieces from dead trees. Thomas chopped some low pine limbs at the bog's edge. I peeled birch bark for a starter.

The ice melted around the log Thomas and I shared. We took off our boots and rested our sock feet on spruce branches almost in the blaze. Our thawing toes hurt. The smoke rose straight in the air. We ate the cans of sardines Mother had tucked in our coat pockets. We shared the roll of Life Savers and strong cheese wrapped in brown paper. The snow did not quench our thirst.

Far down the pond we saw Father chopping with his pick: steady, straight-backed, strong. We could hear the ring of iron on ice.

The mink traps had been empty when we'd followed the brook in to the pond. One was frozen over so a mink could have walked right on it without harm. Father had smashed the ice without a word. He made Thomas reset the trap, plunging bare hands and arms into the black water. Water seeped out from the fire and turned the snow to gray slush at our feet. Cinders floated. I gathered sticks and watched them flame. I held a brand to the back of Thomas's bent neck to make him jump and knock it away. I threw bits of snow into the fire to hear the sizzle.

Thomas huddled over the warmth. "You didn't have to come, you know," I told him.

"Yes, I did," he said with red eyes. Father didn't always have to punish Thomas to bring the redness. Sometimes he just shook his head or set his jaw so the skin was tight, and Thomas would shut up and be red-eyed.

"Are you still cold?" I asked.

"Yes!"

I wished I hadn't asked. I wanted him to say, "'Course not, damn you."

"He won't be much longer," I said.

"You don't know."

Before Father finished the beaver sets, the flakes had started. They were slow and scattered at first so we hardly noticed, picking up to sting our cheeks and melt on our faces.

I watched the swirling against the sky. I welcomed the snow. Thomas watched it accumulate on his sock through the hole in his boot.

"Should we put the fire out, Father?" We refastened our snowshoes. We pulled hats down and scarves up for the long walk home.

"What's it gonna burn in all this snow, little girl?" He struggled to button his coat around his neck, still sweating from work.

Thomas kicked snow on the fire when Father's back was turned.

"Where's it gonna go, Thomas?" I asked.

Father snapped around at us but did not speak. He hurried us. He knew the snow would not stop. The flakes were tiny, fast, wet-falling.

We walked too fast. We walked fast enough to make my side pain and to make Thomas stagger. I watched the tails of Thomas's snowshoes while the snow fell so heavy I could hardly see anything else. I thought we might go straight home and leave the two last fisher traps for another time, but Father left us sitting in the snow while he took the side path up to the first one.

He'd be right back if the trap was empty. If not, the resetting would take some time. The snow piled on Thomas's shoulders. When Father didn't come back and didn't come back, I stomped my feet, clapped my mittens, and danced in the snow. "Come on, Thomas, dance with me. We'll do a snow dance to be warm." Sometimes in our room Thomas and I danced until we were dizzy and red-faced. I could barely see him through the snow, but his words were clear and sharp in the silence of woods where even the birds were hiding until the storm passed. "He's taking his sweet time."

"He must have caught something," I said.

"I don't care," said Thomas.

"You should be glad."

"You gonna be a trapper when you grow up, little girl?" he mimicked.

"Shut up," I said. "I don't know why you're so mad

just because you're cold. There's worse things than being cold."

I would follow Father's trail. I would walk to meet him. I would help. "He told us to stay here. You'd better stay here." Thomas grabbed my wrist at the bare part where mitten didn't meet the cuff. The snow on his mitten stung me.

"I ain't tired," I said. "Are you, Thomas?"

I met Father.

"I told you to wait below," he said. His eyes gleamed.

"What'd you catch?" I asked, knowing.

"A pretty little female, Elizabeth. Peek in the pack." He knelt. Female fisher had the finest fur and brought the best money.

She rested in his basket on top of his traps and ax and scent pouch. I pulled her out and rubbed her back against my face. The fur tickled.

"Can I carry her?"

"Don't drop her or drag her. I don't want no fur rubbed off."

I pulled off my mitten and touched her with my bare hand. The body moved with my pressing, the flesh still soft. Carrying her in my arms, I felt as if I had tamed a wild, living animal.

The snow piled on our snowshoes till we had to kick and push it off. Thomas and I strayed from the trail and tripped on invisible rocks and bushes. Father set too steady a pace. We followed, though, and did not fall far behind because he said not to.

Thomas breathed loud enough for me to hear even at rest. While Father went to tend the final trap, Thomas and I sat close together under a spruce. Father disappeared in the darkness. Night had come early with the storm. The low branches kept the snow from striking us directly. I could smell the spruce needles. The snow bent the branches to the ground.

The fisher lay stretched across my lap, her tail in the snow, her head on Thomas's knee.

"He's not coming back," Thomas said through his scarf. "He's going to leave us here and tell Ma we got lost."

"He might leave you the way you act," I said. "But he wouldn't leave me."

Thomas cried, I think, though I really couldn't see.

"You talk foolish, Thomas. You don't talk like my brother."

"I'm cold," he said.

"Just because you're cold . . . "

"He don't care about us, you know," said Thomas.

"We'll be home pretty soon. You'll thaw."

"He don't!"

"How do you know?"

"It's just the way he is," Thomas said. "He just does what he wants. He don't care about nobody."

I knew lots Father cared about. He cared about Mother because she was his wife. He cared about us because we were his kids. He cared about animals and outwitting them.

I held the fisher's face to mine and rubbed the length of her across my lips. She was warm and quiet. I imagined her my pet. If she'd been alive, though, she'd have been clawing and biting and fighting me. I loved her dead.

"Your mouth flaps too much," I said, the way Father would have said it.

"If we freeze up, he'll be in trouble."

"Why'd he be in trouble 'cause you were so stupid to

freeze yourself? Why'd you want to get your own father in trouble? You're crazy."

"I hate you," he said, and meant it.

I hugged the dead fisher. I started out through the close spruce. My eyes strained to follow the tiny flakes that bent the thick branches. I would watch for Father, and he would come. Snow could not stop him.

Miracle Boy

■ ■ ■

Pinckney Benedict

Lizard and Geronimo and Eskimo Pie wanted to see the scars. Show us the scars, Miracle Boy, they said.

They cornered Miracle Boy after school one day, waited for him behind the shop-class shed, out beyond the baseball diamond, where the junior high's property bordered McClung's place. Miracle Boy always went home that way, over the fence stile and across the fields with his weird shuffling gait and the black-locust walking stick that his old man had made for him. His old man's place bordered McClung's on the other side.

Show us the scars. Lizard and Geronimo and Eskimo Pie knew all about the accident and Miracle Boy's reattached feet. The newspaper headline had named him Miracle Boy. MIRACLE BOY'S FEET REATTACHED IN EIGHT-HOUR SURGERY. Everybody in school knew, everybody in town. Theirs was not a big town. It had happened a number of years before, but an accident of that sort has a long memory.

Lizard and Geronimo and Eskimo Pie wanted to see where the feet had been sewn back on. They were interested to see what a miracle looked like. They knew about miracles from the Bible—the burning bush, Lazarus who walked again after death—and it got their curiosity up.

Miracle Boy didn't want to show them. He shook his head when they said to him, Show us the scars. He was a portly boy, soft and jiggly at his hips and belly from not being able to run around and play sports like other boys, like Lizard and Geronimo and Eskimo Pie. He was pigeon-toed and wearing heavy dark brogans that looked like they might have some therapeutic value. His black corduroy pants were too long for him and pooled around his ankles. He carried his locust walking stick in one hand.

Lizard and Geronimo and Eskimo Pie asked him one last time—they were being patient with him because he was a cripple—and then they knocked him down. Eskimo Pie sat on his head while the other two took off his pants and shoes and socks. They flung his socks and pants over the sagging woven-wire fence. One of the heavy white socks caught on the rusted single strand of bob-wire along the top of the fence. They tied the legs of his pants in a big knot before tossing them. They tied the laces of the heavy brogans together and pitched them high in the air, so that they caught and dangled from the electric line over-head. Miracle Boy said nothing while they were doing it. Eskimo Pie took his walking stick from him and threw it into the bushes.

They pinned Miracle Boy to the ground and exam-ined his knotted ankles, the smooth lines of the scars, their pearly whiteness, the pink and red and purple of the swollen, painful-looking skin around them.

Don't look like any miracle to me, said Eskimo Pie. Miracle Boy wasn't fighting them. He was just lying there, looking in the other direction. McClung's Hereford steers had drifted over the fence, excited by the goings-on, thinking maybe somebody was going to feed them. They were a good-looking bunch of whiteface cattle, smooth-hided and stocky, and they'd be going to market soon.

It just looks like a mess of old scars to me, Eskimo Pie said.

Eskimo Pie and Geronimo were brothers. Their old man had lost three quarters of his left hand to the downstroke of a hydraulic fence-post driver a while before, but that hadn't left anything much to reattach.

It's miracles around us every day, said Miracle Boy.

Lizard and Geronimo and Eskimo Pie stopped turning his feet this way and that like the intriguing feet of a dead man. Miracle Boy's voice was soft and piping, and they stopped to listen.

What's that? Geronimo wanted to know. He nudged Miracle Boy with his toe.

Jesus, he made the lame man to walk, Miracle Boy said. And Jesus, he made me to walk, too.

But you wasn't lame before, Geronimo said. Did Jesus take your feet off just so he could put them back on you?

Miracle Boy didn't say anything more. Lizard and Geronimo and Eskimo Pie noticed then that he was crying. His face was wet, shining with tears and mucus. They saw him bawling, without his shoes and socks and trousers, sprawled in his underpants on the ground, his walking stick caught in a pricker bush. They decided that this did not look good.

They were tempted to leave him, but instead they helped him up and retrieved his socks and unknotted his pants and assisted him into them. He was still crying as they did it. Eskimo Pie presented the walking stick to him with a flourish. They debated briefly whether to go after his shoes, dangling from the power line overhead.

In the end, though, they decided that, having set him on his feet again, they had done enough.

Miracle Boy's old man was the one who cut Miracle Boy's feet off. He was chopping corn into silage. One of the front wheels of the Case 1370 Agri-King that he was driving broke through the crust of the cornfield into a snake's nest. Copperheads boiled up out of the ground. The tractor nose-dived, heeled hard over to one side, and Miracle Boy slid off the fender where he'd been riding.

Miracle Boy's old man couldn't believe what he had done. He shut off the tractor's power-takeoff and scrambled down from the high seat. He was sobbing. He pulled his boy out of the jaws of the silage chopper and saw that the chopper had taken his feet.

It's hard not to admire what he did next.

Thinking fast, he put his boy down, gently put his maimed boy down on the ground. He had to sweep panicked copperheads out of the way to do it. He made a tourniquet for one leg with his belt, made another with his blue bandanna that he kept in his back pocket. Then he went up the side of the silage wagon like a monkey. He began digging in the silage. He dug down into the wet heavy stuff with his bare hands.

From where he was lying on the ground, the boy could see the silage flying. He could tell that his feet were gone. He knew what his old man was looking for up there. He knew exactly.

Miracle Boy's old man called Lizard's mother on the telephone. He told Lizard's mother what Lizard and Geronimo and Eskimo Pie had done to Miracle Boy. He told her that they had taken Miracle Boy's shoes from him. That was the worst part of what they had done, he said, to steal a defenseless boy's shoes.

The next day, Miracle Boy's old man came to Lizard's house. He brought Miracle Boy with him. Lizard thought that probably Miracle Boy's old man was going to whip the tar out of him for his part in what had been done to Miracle Boy. He figured Miracle Boy was there to watch the beating. Lizard's own old man was gone, and his mother never laid a hand on him, so he figured that, on this occasion, Miracle Boy's old man would likely fill in.

Instead, Lizard's mother made them sit in the front room together, Lizard and Miracle Boy. She brought them cold Coca-Colas and grilled cheese sandwiches. She let them watch TV. An old movie was on; it was called *Dinosaurus!* Monsters tore at one another on the TV screen and chased tiny humans. Even though it was the kind of thing he would normally have liked, Lizard couldn't keep his mind on the movie. Miracle Boy sat in the crackling brown reclining chair that had belonged to Lizard's old man. The two of them ate from TV trays, and whenever Miracle Boy finished his glass of Coca-Cola, Lizard's mother brought him more. She brought Lizard more, too, and she looked at him with searching eyes, but Lizard could not read the message in her gaze.

By the third glassful of Coca-Cola, Lizard started to feel a little sick, but Miracle Boy went right on, drinking and watching *Dinosaurus!* with a enraptured expression on his face, occasionally belching quietly. Sometimes his lips moved, and Lizard thought he might be getting ready to say something, but he and Lizard never swapped a single word the whole time.

Miracle Boy's old man sat on the front porch of

Lizard's house and looked out over the shrouded western slope of the Blue Ridge and swigged at the iced tea that Lizard's mother brought him, never moving from his seat until *Dinosaurus!* was over and it was time to take Miracle Boy away.

Geronimo and Eskimo Pie got a hiding from their old man. He used his two-inch-wide black bull-hide belt in his good hand, and he made them take their pants down for the beating, and he made them thank him for every stroke. They couldn't believe it when Lizard told him what his punishment had been. That, Geronimo told Lizard, is the difference between a house with a woman in charge and one with a man.

Lizard saw Miracle Boy's shoes every day, hanging on the electric wire over by McClung's property line, slung by their laces. He kept hoping the laces would weather and rot and break and the shoes would come down by themselves, and that way he wouldn't have to see them anymore, but they never did. When he was outside the school, his eyes were drawn to them. He figured that everybody in the school saw those shoes. Everybody knew whose shoes they were. Lizard figured that Miracle Boy must see them every day on his way home.

He wondered what Miracle Boy thought about that, his shoes hung up in the wires, on display like some kind of a trophy, in good weather and in bad. Nestled together nose to tail up in the air like dogs huddled for warmth. He wondered if Miracle Boy ever worried about those shoes.

He took up watching Miracle Boy in school for signs of worry. Miracle Boy kept on just like before. He wore a different pair of shoes these days, a brand new pair of coal-black Keds that looked too big for him. He shuffled from place to place, his walking stick tapping against the vinyl tiles of the hallway floors as he went.

I'm going to go get the shoes, Lizard announced one day to Geronimo and Eskimo Pie. It was spring by then, the weather alternating between warm and cold, dark days that were winter hanging on and the spring days full of hard bright light. Baseball season, and the three of them were on the bench together. Geronimo and Eskimo Pie didn't seem to know what shoes Lizard was talking about. They were concentrating on the game.

Miracle Boy's shoes, Lizard said. Geronimo and Eskimo Pie looked up at them briefly. A breeze swung them first gently clockwise and just as gently counterclockwise.

You don't want to fool with those, Eskimo Pie said.

Lectrocute yourself, Geronimo said.

Or fall to your doom, Eskimo Pie said.

Lizard didn't say anything more to them. He kept his eyes on the shoes as they moved through their slow oscillation, and he watched the small figure of Miracle Boy, dressed in black like a preacher, bent like a question mark as he moved beneath the shoes, as he bobbed over the fence stile and hobbled across the brittle dead grass of the field beyond.

The trees are beginning to go gloriously to color in the windbreak up by the house. The weather is crisp, and the dry unchopped corn in the field around Miracle Boy and his old man chatters and rasps and seems to want to talk. Miracle Boy (though he is not Miracle Boy yet— that is minutes away) sits on the fender of the tractor, watching his old man.

Soon enough, Miracle Boy will be bird-dogging whitewings out of the stubble of this field. Soon enough, his old man will knock the fluttering doves out of the air with a blast of hot singing birdshot from his 12-gauge Remington side-by-side, and Miracle Boy will happily shag the busted birds for him. When the snow falls, Miracle Boy will go into the woods with his old man, after the corn-fat deer that are plentiful on the place. They will drop a salt lick in a clearing that he knows, by a quiet little stream, and they will wait together in the ice-rimed bracken, squatting patiently on their haunches, Miracle Boy and his old man, to kill the deer that come to the salt.

Lizard made a study of the subject of the shoes. They were hung up maybe a yard out from one of the utility poles, so clearly the pole was the way to go. He had seen linemen scramble up the poles with ease, using their broad climbing slings and their spiked boots, but he had no idea where he could come by such gear.

In the end, he put on the tool belt that his old man had left behind, cinched it tight, holstered his old man's Tiplady hammer, and filled the pouch of the belt with sixtypenny nails. He left the house in the middle of the night, slipping out the window of his bedroom and clambering down the twisted silver maple that grew there. He walked and trotted the four miles down the state highway to the junior high school. It was a cold night there in the highlands of the Seneca Valley, and he nearly froze. He hid in the ditches by the side of the road whenever a vehicle went by. He didn't care for anyone to stop and offer him a ride or ask him what it was he thought he was doing.

He passed a number of houses on the way to the school. The lights were on in some of the houses and off in others. One of the houses was Miracle Boy's, he knew, a few hundred yards off the road in a grove of walnut trees, its back set against a worn-down knob of a hill. In the dark, the houses were hard to tell one from another. Lizard thought he knew which house was Miracle Boy's but he couldn't be sure.

His plan was this: to drive one of the sixtypenny nails into the utility pole about three feet off the ground. Then to stand one-footed on that nail and drive in another some distance above it. Then he would stand on the second nail and drive a third, and so on, ascending nail by nail until he reached the humming transformer at the top of the pole. Then, clinging to the transformer, he imagined, he would lean out from the pole and, one-handed, pluck the shoes from the wire, just like taking fruit off a tree.

The first nail went in well and held solid under his weight, and he hugged the pole tight, the wood rough and cool where it rubbed against the skin of his cheek. He fished in the pouch of nails, selected one, and drove it in as well. He climbed onto it. His hands were beginning to tremble as he set and drove the third nail. He had to stand with his back bent at an awkward angle, his shoulder dug in hard against the pole, and already he could feel the strain grinding to life in his back and in the muscles of his forearm.

The next several nails were not hard to sink, and he soon found himself a dozen feet up, clinging to the pole. The moon had risen as he'd worked, and the landscape below was bright. He looked around him, at the baseball diamond, with its deep-worn base path and crumbling pitcher's mound and the soiled bags that served as bases. From his new vantage point, he noted with surprise the state of the roof of the shop shed, the tin scabby and blooming with rust, bowed and beginning to buckle. He had never noticed before what hard shape the place was in.

He straightened his back and fought off a yawn. He was getting tired and wished he could quit the job he had started. He looked up. There was no breeze, and the shoes hung as still as though they were shoes in a painting. He fumbled another nail out of the pouch, ran it through his hair to grease the point, mashed his shoulder against the unyielding pole, set the nail with his left hand, and banged it home.

And another, and another. His clothes grew grimy with creosote, and his eyes stung and watered. Whenever he looked down, he was surprised at how far above the ground he had climbed.

McClung's Herefords found him, and they stood in a shallow semicircle beneath the utility pole, cropping at the worthless grass that grew along the fence line. This was a different batch from the fall before. These were younger but similarly handsome animals, and Lizard welcomed their company. He felt lonesome up there on the pole. He thought momentarily of Miracle Boy, seated before the television, his gaze fixed on the set, his jaws moving, a half-eaten grilled cheese sandwich in his fingers.

The steers stood companionably close together, their solid barrel bodies touching lightly. Their smell came to him, concentrated and musty, like damp hot sawdust, and he considered how it would be to descend the pole and stand quietly among them. How warm. He imagined himself looping an arm over the neck of one of the steers, leaning his head against the hot skin of its densely muscled shoulder. A nail slithered from his numbing fingers, fell, and dinked musically off the forehead of the lead steer. The steer woofed, blinked, twitched its ears in annoyance. The Herefords wheeled and started off across the field, the moonlight silvering the curly hair along the ridgelines of their backs.

The nail on which Lizard was standing began to give dangerously beneath his weight, and he hurried to make his next foothold. He gripped the utility pole between his knees, clinging hard, trying to take the burden off the surrendering nail as it worked its way free of the wood. A rough splinter stung his thigh. He whacked at the wobbling nail that he held and caught the back of his hand instead, peeling skin from his knuckles. He sucked briefly at the bleeding scrapes and then went back to work, striking the nail with the side of the hammer's head. The heavy nail bent under the force of his blows, and he whimpered at the thought of falling. He struck it again, and the nail bit deep into the pine. Again, and it tested firm when he tugged on it.

He pulled himself up. Resting on the bent nail, he found himself at eye level with the transformer at the pole's top. Miracle Boy's shoes dangled a yard behind him. Lizard felt winded, and he took hold of the transformer. The cold metal cut into the flesh of his fingers. There was deadly current within the transformer, he knew, but still it felt like safety to him. He held fast, shifted his weight to his arms, tilted his head back to catch sight of the shoes. Overhead, the wires crossed the disk of the moon, and the moonlight shone on the wires, on the tarnished hardware that fixed them to the post, on the ceramic insulators. These wires run to every house in the valley, Lizard thought.

He craned his neck farther and found the shoes. Still there. The shoes were badly weathered. To Lizard, they looked a million years old, like something that ought to be on display in a museum somewhere, with a little white card identifying them. SHOES OF THE MIRACLE BOY. The uppers were cracked and swollen, pulling loose from the lowers, and the tongues protruded obscenely. Lizard put a tentative hand out toward them. Close, but no cigar.

He loosened his grip, leaned away from the pole. The arm with which he clung to the transformer trembled with the effort. Lizard trusted to his own strength to keep from falling. He struggled to make himself taller. The tips of his outstretched fingers grazed the sole of one of the shoes and set them both to swinging. The shoes swung away from him and then back. He missed his grip, and they swung again. This time, he got a purchase on the nearest shoe.

He jerked, and the shoes held fast. Jerked again and felt the raveling laces begin to give. A third time, a pull nearly strong enough to dislodge him from his perch, and the laces parted. He drew one shoe to him as the other fell to the ground below with a dry thump. He wondered if the sound the shoe made when it hit was similar to the sound he might make. The shoe he held in his hand was the left.

In the moonlight, Lizard could see almost as well as in the day. He could make out McClung's cattle on the far side of the field, their hind ends toward him, and the trees of the windbreak beyond that, and beyond that the lighted windows of a house. It was, he knew, Miracle

Boy's house. Set here and there in the shallow bowl of the Seneca Valley were the scattered lights of other houses. A car or a pickup truck crawled along the state road toward him. The red warning beacons of a microwave relay tower blinked at regular intervals on a hogback to the north.

Lizard was mildly surprised to realize that the valley in which he lived was such a narrow one. He could easily traverse it on foot in a day. The ridges crowded in on the levels. Everything that he knew was within the sight of his eyes. It was as though he lived in the cupped palm of a hand, he thought.

He tucked Miracle Boy's left shoe beneath his arm and began his descent.

When Lizard was little, his old man made toys for him. He made them out of wood: spinning tops and tiny saddle horses, trucks and guns, a cannon and caisson just like the one that sat on the lawn of the county courthouse. He fashioned a bull-roarer that made a tremendous howling when he whirled it overhead but that Lizard was too small to use; and what he called a Limber Jack, a little wooden doll of a man that would dance flat-footed while his father sang: "Was an old man near Hell did dwell, / If he ain't dead yet he's living there still."

Lizard's favorite toy was a Jacob's Ladder, a cunning arrangement of wooden blocks and leather strips about three feet long. When you tilted the top block just so, the block beneath it flipped over with a slight clacking sound, and the next block after that, and so on, cascading down the line. When all the blocks had finished their tumbling, the Jacob's Ladder was just as it had been before, though to Lizard it seemed that it ought to have been longer, or shorter, or anyhow changed.

He could play with it for hours, keeping his eye sharp on the line of end-swapping blocks purling out from his own hand like an infinite stream of water. He wanted to see the secret of it.

I believe he's a simpleton, his old man told his mother.

You think my boy wants anything to do with you little bastards?

Lizard wanted to explain that he was alone in this. That Geronimo and Eskimo Pie were at home asleep in their beds, that they knew nothing of what he was doing. Miracle Boy's old man stood behind the closed screen door of his house, his arms crossed over his chest, a cigarette snugged in the corner of his mouth. The hallway behind him was dark.

I don't necessarily want anything to do with him, Lizard said. I just brought him his shoes.

He held out the shoes, but Miracle Boy's old man didn't even look at them.

Your mommy may not know what you are, Miracle Boy's old man said, and his voice was tired and calm. But I do.

Lizard offered the shoes again.

You think he wants those things back? Miracle Boy's old man asked. He's got new shoes now. Different shoes.

Lizard said nothing. He stayed where he was.

Put them down there, Miracle Boy's old man said, nodding at a corner of the porch.

I'm sorry, Lizard said. He held on to the shoes. He felt like he was choking.

It's not me you need to be sorry to.

Miracle Boy appeared at the end of the dark hallway. Lizard could see him past the bulk of his old man's body. He was wearing canary-yellow pajamas. Lizard had never before seen him wear any color other than black.

Daddy? he said. The sleeves of the pj's were too long for his arms, they swallowed his hands, and the pajama legs lapped over his feet. He began to scuff his way down the hall toward the screen door. He moved deliberately. He did not have his walking stick with him, and he pressed one hand against the wall.

His old man kept his eyes fixed on Lizard. Go back to bed, Junior, he said in the same tired tone that he had used with Lizard before.

Daddy?

Miracle Boy brushed past his old man, who took a deferential step back. He came to the door and pressed his pudgy hands against the screen. He looked at Lizard with wide curious eyes. He was a bright yellow figure behind the mesh. He was like a bird or a butterfly. Lizard was surprised to see how small he was.

Miracle Boy pressed hard against the door. If it had not been latched, it would have opened and spilled him out onto the porch. He nodded eagerly at Lizard, shyly ducking his head. Lizard could not believe that Miracle Boy was happy to see him. Miracle Boy beckoned, crooking a finger at Lizard, and he was smiling, a strange small inward smile. Lizard did not move. In his head, he could hear his old man's voice, his long-gone old man, singing, accompanied by clattering percussion: the jigging wooden feet of the Limber Jack. Miracle Boy beckoned again, and this time Lizard took a single stumbling step forward. He held Miracle Boy's ruined shoes in front of him. He held them out before him like a gift.

Burn Pile

■ ■ ■

Nancy K. Brown

I was startled awake. The storm had been blowing rain that spit at my windows like gravel propelled from a tire spinning away from a truck stop. After several hours, the constant racket had become familiar. So it wasn't the pelting rain or torn twigs battering our house that had awakened me. I listened for a different sound to stand out above the storm's roar. Then I heard the crack, whoosh, and rumble. I felt the house shudder and I knew what it was—while my family slept up here on the hilltop, another tree had gone down in the woods below.

I knew about storms and storm duty. I had been digging water trenches, tugging downed branches off the roadways all my life. I could find a flashlight by feel. The storms in the Santa Cruz Mountains of California include powerful winds, high creeks, flooding rivers, battered ocean cliffs, and gooey mudslides. Some of our neighbors had tall trees that were close enough to send branches crashing down into their bedrooms, or onto their decks, which snapped off. Our trees weren't near the house, but we had plenty of them in the woods below, around the driveway and along the only road out to the school bus stop. As I slipped back to sleep, I willed the road to be blocked so I wouldn't have to go to school. On the other hand, if there were no school, I'd be spending the whole day doing clean-up and giving a hand to neighbors who needed it.

A silent drizzle welcomed the gray morning. The cat plinked at the wire screen, peering through the reshaped mesh that I had stitched in the corner last summer. I whacked her away with the back of my hand, hitting the stickery edge of the patch. As she darted toward the kitchen, I brought my hand to my mouth to lick away the tiny drops of blood. The power was still out, so we'd eat cold cereal and skip our baths. I could hear my mother in the bathroom sloshing a washcloth in a pan of water. When the power was out, the well pump was, too. And that meant there was one flush left and we'd drink bottled water and heat our wash-up water on the wood-stove. Our neighbors, Mr. and Mrs. Neal, had a generator that came on automatically when the power went out. I could hear the chuffing of its small motor across the canyon. I'd have to remember to call the Neals when the power was restored since they couldn't tell unless it was dark and they could see our lights glowing. The Neals were a middle-aged couple with grown kids and gardens like the ones in town. They were always out there mowing and pulling weeds. Not my family. Our house was surrounded by wild and native vegetation with just a few rhododendrons, azaleas, and dogwoods that we watered only on the hottest days of summer.

The door slammed. Cold air rushed across my bare legs and under my nightie. My dad had returned from checking out the damage. He stood in the hall in muddy boots and dripping jacket and announced in his boom- ing voice, "Everybody get dressed. It's bad out there. We've got some cutting to do. Get those gloves," he told me, "and meet me down by the horse paddock. We're gonna start the burn pile down there this year. We lost five or six fir, two small oaks, and part of our pasture fence. There's branches everywhere. I don't think anyone can get out on the road."

My mom scooted from the bathroom, toweling her wet hair with one hand and clutching thick socks with the other. "Any serious damage that you can see?" she asked as she ducked into her room. After a series of opening and closing drawers, she came into the kitchen in stockinged feet, all dressed, carrying her boots. Her hair was tied into a pony-tail that dribbled water onto her work shirt in a dark stain halfway down her back.

Dad's voice boomed, "What's the point in washing up, Meg? I don't see why you're gettin' clean, just to get dirty." He took the cereal box from my hands, scooped dry cereal in big handfuls, and tossed them into his mouth. Some of the flakes sprinkled all over the floor for the dog to lick up. "There's a skinny redwood leaning on the wires and sparks are shooting out onto the wet pavement. I talked to Jeff and he's already called the power company and put some cones out there to keep folks back. They got work all over the county, and I don't imagine they'll get up here for the few of us on this road until they finish up the big problems. So we'll just have to sit tight. Let's get out there, you two."

We finished our cold cereal, tucked some fruit in our pockets, and filled a jug with water. Then Dad and I headed down the driveway to the lower acreage. I'd packed my wool-clad feet into hiking boots, snapped a yellow slicker over my sweatshirt, and stuffed my hair into a nylon stocking cap. We loaded up the truck with tools, a gas can, and a fresh yellow bale from the garden shed.

"What's the hay for?" I asked Dad.

"Not hay. It's straw. We gotta hold back the mud in a few spots. I want you to sprinkle this around on the slope when we get down there."

My dad really counts on my mom and me to help out. My older brothers both moved away from home a few years ago, one off to college and the other to be married and start a family of his own in Colorado. I'm probably stronger than most fourteen-year-old girls that I know. And I probably can run faster, too. But I have no time for track or basketball because I have too many chores. I made that choice years ago when I got my horse. She became my best friend, my sister, and my only after-school activity. When I'm not riding her on the trails through the mountains near our ranch, I clean her paddock, groom her, and stack her bales of hay. She and her two stablemates take all of my spare time.

I saw my mare braced against the swirling mist, her mane and tail shifting with the direction of the breeze. She probably hadn't slept all night. Horses have to remain vigilant, using their ears and eyes for signs of predators. The flight rather than fight response is strong in horses. Her instincts would have kept her awake, nervously shifting her ears to avoid the howling wind. She'd have been watching for imagined mountain lions or any fierce thing with teeth that might want to bite into her slick, fur-covered meat. The fact is there are few predators who will attack a horse in our area. We do have mountain lions, but they eat rabbits, small deer, and other meaty animals, not big horses. But she doesn't know that. So she caught up on her sleep in the light drizzle, opened her eyes every few seconds, and looked in my direction.

I yanked the bale of straw to the edge of the truck bed, pulled my knife from my pocket, and snapped the three strings. I hugged two wedges at a time, each about five inches thick, and trudged through the mud and up the slope to scatter the straw. I peeled apart each "flake,"—a term used for the separate wedges created at baling—and tossed the pieces in a huge arc, like broadcasting seeds for pasture planting. As I slipped back down, I tried to avoid pulling the damp and slippery soil with me. My boots were caked with it. After several trips, the bale was gone, my slicker plastered with shreds of straw and my woolen socks packed with sticky mud. My dad gestured for me to head on over to the fence line where he had been sawing up a downed oak. It was time to drag it to the burn pile.

Dragging is a kid's job. You can do it when you're just a little kid, a few sticks at a time. As you get stronger you progress to stacking the matted branches like a sled that you add more to. Then you drag it, pull it apart, and heave it toward the pile. When I was little I'd drag, pause, then squat low to search for fancy, ruffled fungus and fluffy moss to make beds for the beetles I'd collected. I wasn't expected to add my branches to the mound, just push them close enough for my mom to grab.

I learned that there was a desired structure to the pile. I'd watch my brothers fight over the proper placement of each addition, arguing about airflow, teepee design, layering, and whether to put heavy branches at the bottom or the top. I don't ever remember my dad giving them the answer. Maybe there wasn't really a right way. As with most things, Dad felt it was important to figure out how to build a burn pile your own way.

There were more hours of dragging than I could ever

finish alone. Mom was restringing wire and digging new post-holes to repair the pasture fence that had been damaged. The horses had been in their paddocks for the night so they hadn't escaped. Not this time anyway. That had happened once before, though. I was twelve at the time and a freak storm had blown a neighbor's tree down onto our fence. The horses must have been really scared, and they took off through the downed fencing. I heard their thundering hooves pounding up the driveway near my room. I had thought I was dreaming, until I heard a neighbor's horse scream in signal from across the canyon. With help from the people whose tree had broken the fence, we managed to head them off and herd them back into the barn for the night. That was one of numerous times during my childhood that Dad had sat down, looked back at an event, and asked all of us to think about "what we could a done different." Mom suggested adding an extra fence around the horse area so we could move them into a smaller paddock each night. That was a good plan. They hadn't gotten out during the storm season even though the fence had been down several times. All I could offer was that I wouldn't have cried.

After our lunch break, the sky cleared and Dad told me to stop dragging so we could burn the pile before it got too big. He drove up to the shop for the diesel can, matches, his felt hat, and a few garden rakes to control the coals. I finished up one last drag, adding dry fir branches from last year under some of the greener oak. I stacked it like a sandwich, a layer of skinny green brush, a layer of hot burning oily bay trees, skinny green, dry fir, then large green to pack it down. I didn't want it to burn away underneath. This way, I knew from experience that the heavy stuff would fall into the hollow where the fast burning brush had turned to coals. I hooked up four hoses from the paddock area and pulled them over to the pile. I took off my cap and tied a scarf on my head. I didn't want my nylon stocking cap to melt if a spark landed on it. I'd ruined a few caps that way. Then I sat back with my arms wrapped around my knees and admired my perfect pile. We all gathered ceremoniously for the lighting.

Dad drizzled diesel fuel on four distinct sides. The pile was a monster, ten feet in each direction beyond the legal limit of four feet high by four feet wide. I got to light it. I struck the small torch, and it exploded into flames. My mom clapped. And I bowed. To toast, Mom and Dad drank a beer and I sucked water from the hose.

I lit all four sides, and when my parents headed back up to the house, I stayed to watch my fire. Only for the last couple winters had I been allowed to tend the fire myself. I was always a little nervous at first, so I walked around it in circles looking for problems, places that might have become hollow, smothered, or dead. Sometimes it just needed to be rearranged, lit again or a branch wiggled to release new sparks. I liked tending as long as I got a break now and then, but I could tell that I wouldn't be able to leave that fire alone for quite a while. I knew that a fire could get itself in trouble quickly.

As the wind died down, the fire popped evenly, sprouting foot-tall flames and breathing at a regular pace. I sat on the log, relaxed, and while peeling my orange stared at the horses through the smoke. Positive, then negative space exchanged places in my vision. A shapely dark boulder became a jigsaw shape, then a boulder again. As I pondered these images, I became aware that something was moving behind the log I was sitting on. I heard a shuffle in the brush. I swiveled around, leaned over, and put my gloved hand into the coyote bush that was dripping with rain and tangled with dormant poison oak stems. A scraggly, wet baby bird ducked its head in a gesture of self-protection. It was a big bird but definitely a baby, and one of its legs was cocked out to the side at an angle.

The orphan was the size of a large grapefruit, bald-headed with sparse gray and brown feathers, beige skin peeking through. It had huge pinkish feet and an over-sized hooked beak. It was shaking with fear, dampness, and chill. I carefully picked it up, avoiding its snapping beak and the fragile broken leg. I rolled it into my sweat-shirt like a burrito and zipped up my slicker. Wrapped in darkness and warmed by my body heat, the fragile crea-ture seemed to calm.

I sang the bird a few songs as I watched the fire. Mom and Dad hadn't returned and there I was caring for a baby, so I sang it a lullaby. I wondered what sounds its mother would naturally make. I tried a few coos and low squawks, but it didn't react. Afraid it couldn't breathe so snugly blanketed, I opened up the damp, warm shirt and allowed the head to stick out. For some reason, I always thought of animals as female until I found out differently, and this bird was no exception. Her big beige beak was so weighty that she rested her head on my sweatshirt. Her yellow eyes rotated, then blinked—they were the eyes of a predator. Her body was shaped like a turkey's, with long legs and a long neck. She must have fallen from her nest during the storm.

I walked around to where Dad had cut up the tree and searched the ground. I saw no signs of a nest. I walked over to the barn, which stood about a hundred feet away from the pile, and got a handful of bran from one of the feed bins. I removed one glove and mixed the bran with some of my warm spit. With mush on my finger, I held it up to her, but her beak stayed shut. Playing mommy bird, I pried open her beak with my gloved hand and wiped the mush onto her pointy tongue with the other. She swallowed, then opened for more. I was feeding her, and she was eating. On the way to get another helping of bran, I poked at the fire, sending a rush of sparks off into the breeze. I pushed my outstretched index finger parallel along the bird's chest, and she grasped both sets of toes around it. That was a good sign. Even her damaged leg was responding. She held onto me tightly with all but two of her toes. The shivering had stopped.

I got a bucket, mixed another handful of bran, some chicken scratch, and a few kibbles of cat food with water, and mashed it. I was using only one hand while the bird gripped the other. Suddenly I noticed my gun. It had hung on the wall of the barn since I last used it in the fall. Nausea crept upward and pushed the orange I'd just eaten into the back of my throat. Last fall I'd gone hunting. I'd killed birds. Birds with feet, feathers, and little bee-bee eyes like the ones on the warm, breathing creature that now studied me as I did her.

My dad was the one to teach me the harder lessons of life. When I was ten years old, he told me that a girl who cried when a snake was killed on the road, as I had just done, wasn't ready to have her own horse—which I'd been begging for.

"You'll be fallin' apart at every little injury, illness, or vet call. I can't see someone as fragile as you taking care of a big animal who's bound to get hurt and will die someday of somethin'. We've got to toughen you up a little," he said. "Let's get you a gun. If you can hunt and clean your own kill, then we'll see about you being a large-animal owner. You gotta' have guts, skill, and smarts livin' in the country."

I blinked away my emerging tears. He was right. I was a sissy. We hopped into his truck and went to get me a shotgun. The gun was a twenty-gauge Charles Daly over-and-under. I spent hours with that gun. I cleaned, loaded, unloaded, and practiced aiming it. I had to work at getting steady enough to aim at cans lined up on a bale of hay. I was giddy with nervous thrill at the power, the noise, and the responsibility of shooting. My biggest challenge was trying to remain on my feet as I shot off a round. It was weird that shotgun pellets flew forward and I flew backward. With a very wide stance, I'd aim and shoot, and soon I could hit my target every time. After each round of shots, the quietness would fill with laughter from my mom and dad, who stood nearby watching me manage the power of the weapon which I had taken to so quickly. I loved the strength that I discovered. And mostly, I loved my dad's reaction.

But my feelings changed when he announced our first hunting trip. When he told me we were going hunting at a duck club, I thought of some funny images—anything to distract myself from the thought of making something bloody and dead. I visualized hundreds of ducks, some lying around on chaise lounges, others paddling or dipping themselves in rippling ponds surrounded by reeds, safe and peaceful. These silly images and childish wishes were not true and I knew it. The real version would include guns, blood, and death. Was that a picture that could possibly include me, a ten-year-old girl who tried to save flies by catching them and tossing them outdoors? All of a sudden I hated my over-and-under.

We slept in the back of the truck in the duck-club parking area. In the morning, when it was still dark, we got up, dressed, ate, and prepared our weapons and shells. I could hear the whispers of other hunters and the clicking of shells as they packed them into plastic boxes and backpacks. Waders with rubber boots were zipped, strapped, and clipped. I could barely see the outlines of the others against the gray-lit sky as we trudged out into the dampness.

Our duck blind was number 24. It was my job to slosh up to each one, check its number, and find ours. The little map we were given was hard to read, and from season to season, as a result of the changing water level, some of the duck blinds had broken apart and disappeared. But after four tries, I found it.

We climbed up onto the wooden platform, which was bordered by reeds on one side and tall bamboo woven into the railing on the other. Hidden from view, we could hear shuffling from other blinds, but no one was supposed to talk. As the sky lit up, the ducks began to quack, then swim out of the reeds; some flapped upward into the navy and pink sky. A few hunters brought eager bird dogs who stood shaking with excitement, making high-pitched whines. Then the shots started. When a duck was hit, the shooter would yell out the number of his blind and the location of the place where the duck fell.

"Number twenty-four, at ten o'clock!" I tumbled down the steps to get the duck my dad shot. He had explained all this to me earlier and I felt ready to do my part. I eagerly sloshed through the swampy slough with the dogs. When I got to the duck, it was dead, but still warm. I didn't look at its face. Its head dropped off to the side and dangled as I made my way back to the blind.

"A nice mallard," Dad said. "Want to gut and clean him right here? They have a plucker and singe machine inside, but I'd like to teach you the old way."

The feathers came out easily, as we pulled. I pulled half a pillowcase full. The down tickled my nose and I sneezed until my dad took over. He cut a slit in the bottom side and I reached in and pulled out the innards. My hands were bloody, smelly, and feathers stuck to them. Among the innards, I felt a hot stretchy bag, the crop, full of seeds from a morning meal. I had to get every little organ and shred of tissue out of the cavity before I could wash up. I gagged twice while cleaning the smaller-than-chicken-sized body. Then I rinsed my hands in the green water in front of the blind and returned to sit with my shotgun aimed into the pale sky.

My stomach lurched and rumbled every time a duck flew overhead. When my chance at a shot came, I passed it up twice. By the third time a duck flew right across my view, I knew I'd better go for it. I hit one on my first try. The duck flapped desperately, then fell to the muddy bank about a hundred yards away.

Dad splashed through the water to it. I cleaned up my sloppy tears and runny nose on my shirt sleeve before he returned. Then he announced, "A beautiful wood duck. Look at this! It must weigh five pounds." I laughed and cried at the same time. So did Dad.

He shot one more duck while I cleaned and plucked the duck I'd killed. I tied its feet to my duck belt and lowered it to let it flop against my hip as we walked back to the clubhouse. I had been so worried about the killing and blood, but now all I could think about was this trophy hanging from my belt for all the other hunters to see. When they came in, boasting about reaching their limit, the size of the ducks, and their good dogs, my dad bragged about me. He and I had hunted every season since.

I poked some of the sticky mixture of grain, cat food kibble, and bran into the little bird's mouth and she pumped her head for more, eagerly swallowing each glob. As I stood to walk back toward the fire, I saw my dad approaching with my lunch. I zipped my slicker to hide the bird.

"Fire looks good, but watch it, the wind is up again." He poked at it a little, then started up his chainsaw. I walked past the hot flames, turning my eyes from the singeing heat, and tapped him to ask if I could take a break and go back to the house. He nodded.

I jogged up the hill, went to my room, and slammed the door. I had to hide this little bird until I was done with the burn pile. Dad was pretty strict about not interfering with nature. Mom always backed him up. But I wasn't sure about this idea. I wondered how it fit with planting trees, cutting trees, and hunting. I padded a shoebox with two pairs of holey socks, put some water in a jar lid, a helping of mash inside, and taped another shoebox on top so the chick would have a little headroom. I put the box in my closet, grabbed a bird identification book from my bookshelf, and ran back down to the pile.

The air was colder and the wind had picked up. With the brush and branches that Dad had added the fire was raging again. Large pieces of glowing ash were propelled into the treetops; the heat was unbearable twenty feet away.

Dad went to help the neighbors across the creek with a downed tree. My mother was at a neighbor-lady's cabin helping get her generator started. I sat by the monstrous, heat-belching fire and browsed through pages and pages of birds. I knew that I had found a predator, not an eagle, hawk, or falcon, but maybe a vulture. There were no pictures of baby birds. I thought if I ever wrote a book like this, I would include pictures of nests, eggs, and chicks. But I read the description and looked carefully at the adult turkey vulture's beak shape and decided that's what my patient was, a turkey vulture.

A large glowing ash dropped onto the page of the book. I was annoyed by the responsibility of the fire and distracted by the bird alone in my room. She needed another feeding with some meat protein. But I knew not to leave the fire unattended. Not in that state.

After another hour, though, the fire seemed calm enough for me to step away for a few minutes. There was a gentle roar from underneath, smoke rose from the embers at the edge of the pile, and the heat had begun to fade. I sprayed the ground with water, left the hose running, and dashed up to the house. I rolled some hamburger, dog kibbles, and sticky rice into a pasty ball, poking it into her mouth. She gobbled it up. I got her to eat three of them. I sucked water up into a straw and drained it into her mouth from mine. She stretched her neck long and high to swallow. I left a marble-sized ball of food for her to eat on her own and taped the box back up. Then I remembered her injury and decided to quickly wrap it. I put two sticks and some tape around her leg to hold the tiny bone together. I set her back in the box, hurried out of the house, and jogged back down to the pile. But before I got there I could see the flames. They had leapt up into the nearest fir tree and caught the whole treetop on fire.

Screaming, I ran back to the house and phoned the neighbor where my mom was working. She had already left. I scrambled onto my bike and flew to where my dad was pulling huge branches through the brush with a couple of other guys. I screamed, "Fire!" And they all ran to the truck, threw my bike in the back, and headed to our place.

I was sobbing by the time we got there. Two trees were on fire and the noise was like a windstorm. They hooked up an emergency fire hose to the tank up on the hill, got our orchard ladder, and Dad stood on the roof of the pickup spraying water toward the flames. The water disappeared into vapor even before it reached the trees. My dad glared at me, then shouted at my mom to call the fire department.

"Can't get a truck in here. Can we?" she shouted back.

Flaky with ashes, pummeled by heat, I sobbed into my lap, my hands clasped over the back of my head and remembered the only other time I had cried this hard. I had left the gate unlatched and the horses had escaped. They ran two miles to the main road and headed toward town. It was a miracle that none of them got injured. I wasn't allowed to ride my horse for two weeks after that. My mom and dad still ask, "Did you latch the gate?" when I return from feeding.

My attention refocused on the smoking and crackling heat and on gruesome thoughts of little animals being singed by a fire that I had caused. I knew this was really, really bad.

Then a helicopter came thwacking up the canyon toward our place with a bucket suspended from the bottom. Someone must have called the Department of Forestry. It dumped a huge bucket of seawater on the trees and doused some of the flames. Fiery debris plunged to the ground and thick steam sent wet ash down on all of us. The fire hissed and squealed as it attempted to revive itself. I took charge of the garden hose and shot at any sign of smoke until each spot sizzled out. The ground seemed alive. It took forever for the helicopter to bring another bucket load. The fire slowly refueled itself, flickering light reflecting on our worried faces. After the second dump of water, the fire squeaked and crackled intermittently and only a few flames remained atop one tree. One more bucket and the spray from our emergency hose took care of the last hot spots.

As the fire's heat began to give way to the coolness of the evening, I sat wrapped in my mom's arms and told her what had happened. When it was nearly dark, the neighbors returned home, and so did we. I retreated to the bathroom. Bathing in a shallow teapot bath with a small flashlight perched on the counter, I wondered what kind of punishment my parents would invent for someone who had set fire to the woods? I knew that I was to blame.

Before dinner, my dad and I walked through a light shower of rain down to the pasture area to check the burn pile. None of us would sleep until every spark was doused. The smell of smoke and ashes greeted as we approached.

The mound was wet through the middle, gummy and steaming. "We could have lost everything, you know. We were real lucky this time. Tell me," he said, "what was so important that you left that pile?"

"I found a bird, Dad." I gathered courage. "It's a turkey vulture chick that fell from a nest." Then I began to explain, "I went up to the house to feed it. I had put it in my closet." Ours eyes locked. Then quickly, I glanced away and looked down at my feet. "I'm really sorry. It was so stupid of me to do that." I sighed, slowly lifting my head to check his face. He was looking off into the woods.

"It sure was stupid." Then it was his turn to look down, scraping his boot back and forth through the wet, sticky ashes.

The horses whinnied for their feed. Leaving Dad with his thoughts, I picked my way through the mud to the feed shed and separated four flakes of hay. I stacked all four flakes on my forearms and pulled them in close. I dropped a flake into each feeder and brushed the flecks of ash from the back of each horse.

Dad stood with his legs stiffly set and his arms tucked around himself as I approached. "I did something pretty stupid myself," he said. He cleared his throat and gained volume. "When I stopped by to check the pile and you weren't here, I added a few more branches that I took off the upper road. I pulled them out of the truck and tossed them onto the pile. I was about to go get you, but it was lookin' pretty calm, so I went back to help the guys. I thought you'd be right back." I sighed and released the breath I'd held tensely all evening, as I realized that Dad had told me that he, too, was responsible for the fire. He sat down on the log and wrapped his head in his arms.

"Dad, " I offered after a while, "I think we both know what we could have done different."

"Yes, I think you're right. I wouldn't want to relive this day for anything, but I'll tell you something, there's plenty here to think on." He stood, grabbed my shoulder, and pulled me in close. Tears pushed to the surface. We surveyed the burn site. The darkened brush and silhouettes of the two charred trees stood as reminders of the day's near-disaster, the pile gently steamed, and the horses snorted and chewed their hay. "Let's see that ugly little bird. You think it's really a vulture?"

"Yes. I found it in my book." Relieved, I slipped my hand into his and we walked back up to the house. I relaxed a little, comforted by the warmth of his hand and the familiar odor of his sweaty body and matched the rhythm of his footsteps.

We pulled open the closet door and peeked into the box. He reached down and picked up the chick. "Dad, please don't make me put her back out there. She's doing well. She has a broken leg and . . . "

"Nice work." He interrupted. "Let's make a splint that supports this joint, here. See?" He gently pulled off the tape I'd wrapped around her bent leg. With his pocketknife, he whittled the stick to a better angle and wrapped it again. He asked me to get a small light bulb from the broom closet to keep her warm and he brought a cord and socket and a bigger box from the garage.

As he bent over the box, the light reflected his kind face. Tears fell down my cheeks. I remembered the time my dad gently wrapped the dog's leg after a coon attack. I could see him plucking the feathers from my first wood duck, and I remembered the way he had looked at me today during the fire. He had tears in his eyes each of those times, yet as quickly as they sprang forth, they were gone. Maybe tears aren't so bad, after all. I turned my head and wiped the trickle of wetness from my face.

We carried the large box into the kitchen. My mom suggested that I add egg to her mash. We all laughed at the sight of me feeding this skin-headed vulture wrapped in my rosebud baby nightgown.

After three weeks, the vulture got huge. I took her to school and we observed her in science class. She lived in an old television box, growing to be a little larger than a chicken with long muscled legs and a giant wingspan, and kept her bald head. Her wings feathered up, her leg healed, and she ate absolutely everything. The kids fed her insects, worms, bologna, potato chips, frozen hamburger meat, and leftover scrambled eggs. When she started flapping as if she wanted to fly, my teacher and several of us kids took her out to the edge of town to release her. Mom met us there. Dad arrived with a camera. The bird hopped out of the box, walked, then ran to the edge of the rocky cliff and flew for the first time. She flapped awkwardly, then smoothed out and glided upward. We all clapped in celebration.

For several weeks I put hamburger out on the rock for her. The vulture flew down and pulled it out of the package as I backed away. When she stopped coming, I assumed she had figured out how to hunt for herself, savoring the flavor of rotting flesh after having put up with grocery-store meat for so long. I understand, because the opposite happened for me. I stopped hunting. So did Dad. Yet sometimes we missed the flavor of fresh-killed, wild duck stuffed with celery, onion, and thyme.

Sugar Among the Chickens

■ ■ ■

Lewis Nordan

I had been fishing for an hour and still hadn't caught anything. I was fishing for chickens. Mama wouldn't let me walk to the town pond by myself. What else was I going to fish for?

I looked back over my shoulder through the torn-out screened door and tried to see Mama in there. I said, "Mama." I was using the voice that says you're being real good and not fishing for chickens.

Mama said, "You better not be fishing for chickens, Sugar Mecklin, you going to get switched." She's got this ability.

She was out in the kitchen, that was good anyway. I put a fresh kernel on my hook and scattered shelled corn on the slick dirt yard below the porch and dusted off my hands on my white blue jeans. A handful of old hens came bobbing and clucking up to the corn and poked at it with their heads and then raised their heads up and looked around, and then started poking at it again.

I dropped the baited hook in amongst them. I wished I could figure out some way to use a cork. The chickens bobbed and pecked and poked and scratched. I moved my baited hook into the middle of the chickens and eased it down onto the ground and waited. I still didn't get a bite.

My daddy didn't much care whether I fished for chickens or not. My daddy knew I never would catch one, never had, never would. It was my mama who was the problem. She said it would ruin your life if you fished for chickens.

I wasn't studying ruining my life right now. I was thinking about hooking and landing some poultry.

I wasn't using a handline, which is easy to hide if your mama comes up on you. I was using a cane pole and a bream hook, little bitty rascal of a hook. I liked a handline all right, I wasn't complaining. Nothing better for fishing in real tight places, like up under your house on a hot day when the chickens are settled down in the cool dirt and have their neck feathers poked out like a straw hat and a little blue film of an eyelid dropped down over their eyes. A handline is fine for that. A cane pole is better from off your porch, though.

Or I guessed it was. I never had caught a chicken. I had had lots of bites, but I never had landed one, never really even set the hook in one. They're tricky, a chicken.

I really wanted to catch one, too. I wanted the hook to snag in the beak, I wanted to feel the tug on the line. I wanted to haul it in, squawking and heavy and beating its wings and sliding on its back and flopping over to its breast and dragging along and the neck stretched out a foot and a half and the stupid old amazed eyes bright as Beau dollars.

I dreamed about it, asleep and awake. Sometimes I let myself believe the chicken I caught was not just any old chicken but maybe some special one, one of the Plymouth Rocks, some fat heavy bird, a Leghorn, or a blue Andalusian. And sometimes, as long as I was making believe, I thought I might catch an even finer specimen, the finest in the whole chicken yard. I thought I caught the red rooster itself.

The red rooster was a chicken as tall as me. It seemed like it, I swear, when I was ten. It was a chicken, I'm telling you, like no chicken you ever saw before. It could fly. There was no half-assed flying about it. It could fly long distance. Daddy said it could migrate if it had anywhere to go. It couldn't do that, but it could fly fifty times farther than any other chicken you ever saw. This was a chicken that one time killed a stray dog.

I dreamed about that rooster. The best dream was when I caught it not on a handline and not on a cane pole. I dreamed I caught it on a limber fine six-and-a-half-foot Zebco rod and spinning reel, like the ones in the Western Auto store in Arrow Catcher. That's the town I used to live right outside of when I was little, in the Delta. The line on that Zebco spool was almost invisible.

I watched the chickens. There was a fine old Plymouth Rock I would just love to catch. She dusted her feathers and took long steps like a kid wearing his daddy's hip boots. I moved the bait closer to her and held my breath. She started poking around at the corn. She hit the bait once but didn't pick up the hook. My line was taut, so I felt the strike vibrate through the line and down the cane pole to my hands, which I noticed were sweating. I thought, If she hit it once, she just might . . . But she didn't. She stopped eating corn altogether and scratched herself with her foot like a dog.

I tried to listen to my mama. Mama couldn't be expected to stay in the kitchen forever. I needed to say something to her in my I-ain't-fishing-for-chickens voice, but I couldn't. The Plymouth Rock pecked the earth a few times, but not the bait. Then, all of a sudden, she shifted position a little and pecked right down on the corn with the hook in it, the bait. For the second time that day I felt a strike vibrate through my hands. But the chicken missed the hook again and I jerked the bait out of her mouth. She didn't know what happened to it. She looked like, What in the world?

I repositioned the bait, and the hen started pecking around it again. I had to say something to Mama. I held real still and tried to talk in a voice that maybe a chicken couldn't hear. In my head I invented a voice that seemed like it was going to be all throaty and hoarse and animallike when it came out, but when it did come out, it didn't make any sound at all, not even a whisper, just a little bit of released breath and a wormy movement of my lips. I said, "Mama, I ain't fishing for chickens." Nobody heard it, not even me. The Plymouth Rock hit the bait a third time.

It wasn't possible to catch a chicken. I knew that. My daddy had convinced me. He said, "A chicken is dumb, but not dumb enough." So I knew it was impossible. But I also knew it had happened. I had the Plymouth Rock.

I jerked my pole skyward and set the hook hard in the chicken's beak.

The sound that rose up out of the chicken's throat was a sound that nobody who has never caught a chicken on a hook has ever heard. It sounded like chicken-all-the-way-back-to-the-beginning-of-chicken.

I was anchored to the porch, with the butt end of the pole dug into my groin for support. The heavy, flopping squalling bird was hanging off the end of my line in midair. The sound didn't stop. The sound was like the fire siren in Arrow Catcher. As beautiful and as scary as that. It was like a signal. I thought it signaled danger and adventure and beauty.

I was screaming too, along with the chicken. I didn't even know I was screaming. I heaved on the heavy bird. The pole was bent double. I wanted to land the chicken. I wanted the Plymouth Rock on the porch with me.

I couldn't pick it up high enough. It was too heavy for me. It was up off the ground, all right, but I couldn't get it high enough to sling it onto the porch. The chicken was beating its wings and spinning in a wild circle. I held it there.

I heaved on the pole again. The bird swung up and around, but was still not high enough. It hit the side of the house and then swung back out into midair.

Mama came out on the porch and stood behind me. I knew she was back there, because I heard the door slap shut.

At first I didn't look back. I just stopped hauling on the chicken. I was still holding it up off the ground, though. I couldn't give it up yet, not all of it, even though I had stopped trying to land it.

Finally I did look back. The face of my mama, I thought, was the saddest face on this earth. It just had to be. I said, "Hey, Mama," real subdued, trying not to provoke her. I was still holding the chicken off the ground, and it still hadn't stopped making its noise. I said, "I been fishing for chickens." No use lying about it now.

I expected my mama to say, "I swan," like she always said when she meant "I swear." What she really said surprised me. She said she was a big failure in life. She said she was such a big failure in life she didn't see why she didn't just go off and eat some poison.

I eased the chicken down to the ground. It got loose and scooted off toward the garage with its feathers sticking out.

Mama cut a switch off a crape myrtle and switched me good on my bare legs and went back inside the house. She lay across her bed on the wedding-ring quilt my grandmama Sugar gave her when she got married, with hers and Daddy's names sewed in a corner and a heart stitched around the names, and had herself a long hard cry. And so that part of it was over.

Some time passed. Some days and, I guess, some weeks. I watched my mama around the house. At night, after supper, and after she had wiped the table, she would do what she liked best. She would lay out on the table a new piece of cloth from Kamp's Low Price Store and pin to it a tissue-paper Simplicity pattern. She would weigh the pattern down all around with pieces of silverware from the dark chest lined with green felt. The silver came from my mama's grandmama who lost her mind and threw away the family Bible and almost everything else and so left only the silverware, which she forgot to throw away. Mama would get the pattern all weighted down, and she would look around for a minute, in her sewing basket or in a kitchen drawer, and say, "Has anybody seen my good scissors?" She would find the scissors and bring them to the table and cut through the paper and the cloth. She would poke through her sewing basket. I saw the faded pincushion and the cloth measuring tape and a metal thimble and about a jillion buttons and the pinking shears.

She would lay down a towel to keep from scratching the dining room table and then heft the heavy old portable Kenmore onto it. She might have to thread the bobbin. She might lift the cloth to her nose and breathe its new-smell before she put it into the machine, under the needle, and on the shiny metal plate. She would touch the pedal with her foot.

Before any of this would happen, before supper even, my daddy would come home from work. I could hear the car pull into the drive and head around back of the house. He would get out of the car, and he would be wearing white overalls and a paper cap with the name of a paint store printed on it. He would smell like paint and turpentine and maybe a little whiskey.

Daddy would shoo the chickens back from the gate in the fence where the chickens would flock when they heard his car. He would open the gate and ease inside, real quick, before anybody could get out. I would watch him.

The chickens were gossipy and busy and fat and fine. Daddy would scatter shelled corn from a white metal dishpan and pour out mash for those that needed it and run well water into the troughs.

I always wished Mama would watch him do this. I thought that if she did she would stop thinking she was a big failure in life.

I went down the steps and into the chicken yard with him. He let me reach my hand into the fragrant dusty corn and pelt the old birds with it.

Then there was the part where the rooster attacks you. Every day I forgot it was going to happen, and then it would happen, and then it would happen and I would think, Now why didn't I remember that?

It happened today, this particular day, I mean, a Tuesday and just before sunset. The rooster was on top of us. It hadn't been there before, and now it was all I could see, the red furious rooster. Its wings were spread out and its bones were creaking and clacking and its beak was wide open and its tongue was blazing black as blood. And the rooster's eye—it looked like it had only one eye, and the eye was not stupid and comical like the other chickens'. It seemed lidless and magical, like it could see into a person's heart and know all his secrets and read his future. And the feet—they were blue-colored, but blue like you never saw before except in a wound. And the spurs.

And then it was over. Today, like other days, Daddy kicked the chicken in the breast with the toe of his work shoe and it flopped over on its back. It righted itself and stood up and started pecking at the corn on the ground. Daddy walked over to the rooster and petted its neck. The bird made a stretching motion with its head like a cat.

Then there was the next part. We watched the rooster eat. Without warning, as we knew it would, it stopped eating. It stood straight up and cocked its head so far that the comb flopped over. It looked like somebody who had just remembered something real important.

Then the rooster took off. Any other flying chickens you see are all hustle and puffing and heaving and commotion and getting ten feet maybe, no matter how hard they work at it. This chicken could fly like a wild bird, like a peacock, maybe, or a wild turkey. There was nothing graceful about it, nothing pretty. It was just so amazing to watch. When the rooster flew, it looked like some fat bad child who has rung your doorbell and is running down the street away from your house, slow and obvious and ridiculous, but padding on anyway, uncatchable. It flew out and out, over the chicken-yard fence, over a little side yard where Mr. Love kept a goat, over the trailer the midgets lived in, out farther like a kite, over a house, and finally into the branches of a line of hardwood trees across the railroad tracks.

We went inside the house then, and Daddy went into the bathroom and came out after a long time with his new smells of Wildroot and Aqua Velva and his wet combed hair. The whiskey smell was a little stronger, a little sweeter.

After supper, and after the sewing machine was turned off and put away, Mama said, "Now all I have to do is hem it, and it'll be all done." She was on the sofa, so she sat up straight and held the dress up to her front and pretended like she was modeling it. Daddy was moving out of the room. He was weaving a little when he walked, on his way to the kitchen.

I looked at Mama. She had a pleased look on her face that made me think she thought she looked pretty. She did look kind of pretty.

I picked up the package the pattern came in. There was a color picture of two women on it. I said, "Where do these ladies live, Mama?"

She took the package out of my hand and looked at it with the same look on her face. She looked off somewhere away from my eyes and said, "I think maybe these two ladies live in New York City. They live across the hall from one another in a penthouse apartment. I think they just met up downtown by accident." She looked at me and smiled and handed the pattern package back to me.

I said, "What are they talking about?"

Mama said, "Hm." She took the package from me again and looked at it, serious. She said, " I think maybe, well, maybe the lady in the red dress is saying why don't we go somewhere real nice today. She's saying why don't they shop around a little and then maybe go to a picture show. They might even be talking about going to the opera, you don't know."

I tried to think about the opera, men in turbans and women in white-powdered wigs. The men carried sabers at their sides, and the women had derringers in their purses. I said, "I ain't studying no opera."

Mama laid the package down and put the dress aside too. She started poking through her sewing basket for something but then stopped without finding it. She had lost the look she had before.

I said, "Are you going to the opera?"

She said, "No."

I said, "When you put on that dress, you know what?"

She didn't answer.

I said, "You ain't going to look like neither one of those ladies." I don't know why I said that.

Mama got up from where she was sitting. She said, "Don't say *ain't,* Sugar. It will ruin your life." She got up off the sofa and went into the bedroom and closed the door.

Daddy came back into the living room. He was wobbly and ripe with whiskey. He said, "What happened to Mama?"

I said, "She's lying down."

He eased back into his chair and started to watch "Gilligan's Island" on the television.

I went to my room. I sat on the bed and let my feet hang off. I had to do something. I felt like I was working a jigsaw puzzle with my family. I saw my mama and my daddy and the chickens and the midgets and Mr. Love's goat and I thought I could never get it worked.

I started to fish for the rooster. Sometimes I fished with a handline, sometimes with a cane pole. The rooster never looked at my bait.

I fished every day, and every day I got older and the rooster didn't get caught. School started up again and I got new shoes. The leaves finally fell off the trees and I helped Mama rake them up in the afternoons. The rooster hated my bait. He couldn't stand to look at it.

I changed bait. I used raisins. I used jelly beans. I used a dog turd. You got to want to catch a chicken to bait a hook with dog turd. Chickens eat them all the time, no reason it wouldn't work. It didn't though.

I threw the cat in the chicken yard. I had ten hooks dangling off the cat, feet and tail and flea collar, everywhere you can put a hook on a cat. The rooster killed the cat, but it didn't take a hook. Too bad about the cat. You're not going to catch a rooster without making a sacrifice or two.

After a while fishing for the rooster and keeping Mama from knowing about it became like a job, like an old habit you never would think about breaking. All that mattered was that I fish for him, that I never give up, no matter how hopeless, no matter how old or unhappy I got.

Something happened then that changed things. It was Saturday. I got on my bike and pedaled from my house to the picture show in Arrow Catcher. There was always a drawing at the matinee.

Mrs. Meyers, the old ticket-taker-upper with the white hair and shaky hands and snuff-breath—she would do the same thing every time. She would take your ticket out of your hand and tear it into halves and tell you what a fine young man you were growing up to be and to hold on to your ticket stub, you might win the drawing.

I walked down the aisle and found me a seat up close to the front. I looked at the torn ticket in my hands, and the other seats filled up with people.

Mr. Gibbs owned the picture show, called it the Strand Theater. The lights were all on bright and Mr. Gibbs climbed up on the stage by a set of wooden steps around the side. He was huffing and sweating, waving his hands for everybody to be quiet. Like he said every Saturday, he said, "Be quiet, boys and gulls, be quiet, please." We laughed at him, and the underarms of his white shirt were soaked with sweat.

I watched Mr. Gibbs crank the handle of a wire basket filled with ping-pong balls. Every ball had a number on it. Mr. Gibbs would draw them out, one at a time, and put each one on a little cushioned platform with the number facing out to the audience, until he had four of them. He would draw them out slow and teasing and smiling. It was something he loved to do, you could tell. He would call out each number in its turn, real loud and exaggerated. He would say, "Fo-urrr," or "Nye-unn," and he would hold up the white ball and show everyone he wasn't cheating, and then he would put the ball on the cushioned stand. You had to like Mr. Gibbs.

Then it started happening. The first number he called

out was the first number on my ticket stub. And then so was the second. It seemed impossible that the number in my ear was the same number as in my eye. It kept on being the same number, digit by digit, right down to the end. I had won the drawing.

I had never won anything before. One time I won a pink cake in a cakewalk. It tasted terrible and I hated it, but I ate all of it anyway, same night I won it. I had never won anything except that cake, so it was impressive enough to win the drawing.

But winning was nothing compared to the prize I was going to take home. I had won the Zebco rod and spinning reel from the Western Auto.

Mr. Gibbs was standing up on that little stage like a sweaty fat angel. He was giving his heartfelt thanks to the Western Auto store, home-owned and home-operated by Mr. Sooey Leonard, and to all the other fine local merchants of Arrow Catcher who donated these fine prizes and made these drawings possible.

I went up on the stage. I climbed the same dusty wooden steps that Mr. Gibbs had climbed. I showed Mr. Gibbs my ticket stub. I was trembling. He shook my hand, and my hand was sweaty and slick against his manly palm and fingers. Mr. Gibbs asked me if I didn't think every single person in this fine audience ought to take his patronage to the Western Auto store and all the other fine local merchants of Arrow Catcher.

I said, "Yessir," and everybody laugh and clapped their hands.

Mr. Gibbs said what was I going to do with my fine prize.

I said, "Go fishing," and everybody laughed again.

Mr. Gibbs said why didn't everybody give this fine

young fisherman another round of applause, and so everybody did.

I don't know what was on the movie. I sat through it, and I watched it, with the fishing rod between my legs, but I didn't see it. I remember a huffing train and some wreckage, I remember an icy train platform and taxicabs and a baby growing up rich instead of poor. Barbara Stanwyck married John Lund, I remember that. Whatever was on the movie, one thing was all I was thinking about and that was that I was definitely going fishing, no doubt about it. The fish I was going to catch was as tall as me and had red feathers and was big enough and fine enough to ruin the life of every soul in Arrow Catcher, Mississippi.

I looked back at the day I caught the rooster. I see the familiar yard, the fence of chicken wire. I smell the sweet fresh fragrance of grain and mash and lime and chickenshit and water from a deep well poured through troughs of corrugated metal. I smell creosote and the green pungent shucks of black walnuts under the tree. I see myself, a boy, holding the Zebco rod I won at the Strand Theater. The Zebco moves back, then whips forward.

The line leaps away from the reel, from the rod's tip. It leaps into S's and figure eights. It floats like the strand of a spider's web. At the end of the line I see the white fleck of sunlight that covers the hook: the bait, the kernel of corn. I watch it fly toward the rooster.

I look ahead of the corn, far down the chicken yard, and see the rooster. It seems to be on fire in the sunlight. For one second I lose my mind and believe that the rooster means something more than a rooster. I don't believe it long. I come to my senses and know that the rooster is a chicken, that's all. A very bad chicken. He is the same miserable wretched mean bad son-of-a-bitch that my daddy has called him every day of the rooster's life. I remember that the rooster is smarter than me, and faster and strong and crazier. I remember that I am in the chicken yard with him and he doesn't like me and that my daddy ain't home from work to protect me and my ass is in trouble, Jack.

I understand, at last, what the rooster is going to do. He is going to catch the bait in the air, like a dog catching a Frisbee. I can't believe what I am watching. The rooster has positioned itself, flat-footed, with its mouth open, its head cocked to one side. Until this moment I have not believed I would catch the rooster. I have meant to catch it, but the habit of fishing for it is all I have thought about for a long time. And now, in the presence of an emotion something like awe, I understand that the rooster is about to catch me.

It happens. The rooster, at the last moment, has to lurch a step forward, it has to duck its head, but it does so with perfect accuracy. The bird might as well have been a large red-feathered frog plucking a fly from the air. He catches the baited hook in his mouth.

I do not move to set the hook. There is no point. The rooster has been fishing for me for three years, and now it has caught me. I have become old enough to believe that doom will always surprise you, that doom is domestic and purrs like a cat.

The bird stands quiet with the bait in its mouth. The line droops to the ground from his chicken lips. I stand attached to him by the line. It is no help to remember that the rooster is a beast and without humor.

Then it does move. At first I thought the creature was growing taller. Nothing could have surprised me. I might have been growing smaller. Neither was true. I was watching what I had watched many times. I was watching the rooster take flight.

It left the ground. The hook was still in its mouth, attached to nothing. The rooster was holding the hook in its mouth like a peanut.

More than ever the bird seemed on fire. It flew out and out, away from me. The nylon line trailed it in flight. The sun shone on the rooster and on the line and told me that I was in big trouble and had not yet figured out how.

It flew over the chicken-yard fence, over the goat, over the midgets. It gained altitude. I watched the line be stripped in coils form my open-faced reel. The bird flew and flew, high as the housetops, and then the tree-tops, out toward the railroad tracks. I was a child flying a living kite.

It took me a minute to see what the rooster was up to. I had never seen him do this before. Just when he was almost out of sight, out over the railroad tracks and ready, I thought, to light in the hardwood trees, the bird seemed to hang suspended. It seemed to have hung itself in midair and to have begun to swell out like a balloon. I was holding the fishing rod limp in my hand and studying the rooster's strange inflation. The rooster, above the treetops, ballooned larger and larger. It grew large enough that I could distinguish its particular features again, the stretched neck and popped-out eyes, the sturdy wings and red belly feathers. Nothing about the appearance of the rooster made sense.

And then everything did. I was not looking at the

bird's tail-feathers, as I should have been. I was looking him in the face. He was not growing larger, he was coming closer. I looked at my reel and saw that the line was still. The rooster had turned around in flight and was coming back after me.

I looked at him. The rooster had cleared the goat and the midgets. It was big as a goose, big as a collie. Its feet were blue and as big as yard rakes. I dropped the fishing rod into the dirt. I turned to the gate and tried to open the latch. I could hear the rooster's bones creaking and clacking. I could hear the feathers thudding against the air. My hands were clubs, the gate would not come unlatched. I pounded at the gate.

I heard the rooster set its wings like a hawk about to land on a fence post. The rooster landed on my head. It didn't fall off. I thought it might, but it did not. It clung to my scalp by its fierce toenails. I clubbed at the gate with my useless hands. The bird stood on my head, and its wings kept up their motion and clatter. I could not appreciate the mauling I was receiving by the wings for the fire the feet had lit in my brain. I tried to climb the gate, but my feet had turned to stumps.

The chicken yard was in hysterics, the Plymouth Rocks and Leghorns and blue Andalusians. I clung to the gate with the rooster on my head. I imagined flames the shape of an angry chicken rising from my head.

I screamed, and still the rooster held on. It drubbed me with its wings. My eyes were blackened and swollen, my nose ran with blood. I didn't care, so long as someone put out the fire in my scalp.

I got the idea that it could be put out with water. I gave up at the gate and ran stumbling across the chicken yard. Layers and pullets and bantams, all the curious and hysterical, fanned away from me in droves. The rooster hung on.

I reached the hydrant hopeless. There was no hope of putting my head under the spigot while wearing the chicken. There was a garden hose in the old garage, but it was of no use. If I could not open the simple latch of the gate, there was no chance I could retrieve the garden hose from its wall hook and screw it to the spigot.

My mama was standing on the back porch watching. I longed for the days when I was young enough to be switched with crape myrtle. I saw her start to move toward me. She was moving toward me but I knew she would never reach me in time. Blood and chickenshit ran down the sides of my face and into my ears. The wings kept up the pounding, and the rooster's bones and ligaments kept up the creaking and clacking and clicking.

I had not noticed my daddy drive up, but now I saw his car in the driveway. He left the car and was headed toward me. He also moved in slow motion.

I left the spigot. My motion and my parent's motion had become the same. They stood at the gate and pounded at it. Their hands were clubs too and the gate would not open for them.

I motioned for them to stay where they were. They saw that I knew what I was doing. Something had changed in me. I was not running now. The rooster was still riding my head. I walked, purposeful, like a heavy bear through the chicken yard.

And yet my steps were not heavy. My life was not ruined. I could wear this chicken on my head forever. I could bear this pain forever. In a year no one would notice the chicken but myself. Then even I would not notice. My mama had believed that spending your life in the place of your birth, absorbing its small particulars into your blood, was ruination. I looked at my parents beside the gate. My daddy held my mama in his arms as they looked at me. My daddy had gotten the gate open now but again I held up my hand and stopped him. I knew now what I could give them. It was a picture of myself that I would live the rest of my life to prove true: they watched their son wear this living crowing rooster like a crown.

They were proud of me. I knew they were. They were frightened also but pride was mainly what I saw in their faces as I kept them from helping me. They believed that my life would not be ruined. They believed that a man who has worn a chicken on his head—worn it proudly, as I was beginning to do—would never be a fool to geography or marriage or alcohol.

I stood tall in the chicken yard. My parents looked at me from the gate and I felt their love and pride touch me. They believed that a man and his wife with such a son could not be ruined either, not yet, not forever.

The rooster had stopped flapping its wings. It was heavy on me, but I straightened my back and did not slump. Now it balanced itself with more ease, it carried more of its own weight and was easier to hold. It stood on my head like an eagle on a mountain crag. I strode toward my parents and they toward me. The three of us, and the rooster, moved through the chicken yard in glory.

The Elevator Man

■　■　▪■

Jon Volkmer

Some said it was corn killed a man first. Tim's dad said
it had something to do with that particular smell of
corn. Like coughing up lungfuls of Green Giant creamed
style, he said. Wilmer figured beans was the worst. You
don't get your big clouds of dust with soybeans, he'd
say, but there was something kind of oily the way it
stuck to your throat and lungs. Wheat was bad.
Everybody knew wheat was bad, but around southern
Otoe County it was mostly hard red winter wheat, and
when you're harvesting around Fourth of July you're too
hot to worry much about dust.

Tim knew milo was worst of all. He was only twelve,
but he had Vaughn Jones to back him up. Vaughn had
operated the grain elevator over in Talmadge for fifty-
one years before he retired and moved to Julian. Tim
saw him shuffle past every day on his way to get his mail
at the store, pulling that oxygen bottle on little wheels
behind him. When Vaughn Jones pointed to the cloud
of red dust raising up out of the back end of the truck
when the milo was pouring in, shook his head, and said
that was the most killing grain dust there was, you had
to believe it. Vaughn said milo didn't have civilized uses
like your corn, wheat, and beans, making bread and like
that. Milo was just your basic hog feed.

They were emptying the south bins at the Julian elevator. Three of them, eighteen feet high and fourteen across, corrugated tin cylinders with Chinese-coolie-hat roofs. Had to get at them in high summer when the ground at the south end wasn't too marshy and would hold the truck, Tim's dad said. That milo had been in there seven years, he said, it was turning into dirt.

Tim sat against the side of the bin, in the shade, watching the auger work. It was a big pipe set up on wheels, with a screw inside, sharp and shiny, that pulled the grain in at the bottom end, propelled it up the pipe, and shot it down into the truck with a tremendous racket.

The red dust churned from the truck and hung like disease in the air. It drifted across the road, turning the white gravel red and coloring the first rows of Wilmer's sweet corn patch with a coppery film. It covered the hood of the truck, the roof, it drifted in through the open windows and settled on the seats, the dash, the black gearshift knob.

When the grain was piled high and almost spilling over on the cab, Tim sprinted into the dust cloud, slid in the seat, and cranked the starter. He moved the truck a few feet ahead, shut her off, and went back upwind to the shade. As he waited for the back end to fill, the heavy rumble of the auger changed to a loud clanking. The clanking stopped for a few seconds, then came back, clattering louder than before. His father came running from the office and killed the juice at the breaker box.

"Don't you know nothing? You can't run her empty. You'll burn out the auger bearings."

His father rapped on the steel door above the hole that fed the auger, listening. He opened the highest of three inner doors, and cursed in the musty smell of milo and pesticide that enveloped them. Peering around his father, Tim saw a high circular wall of grain sloping steeply down to the base of the door. The wall was not even, but molded into grotesque formations, with ridges and crevasses and strange, gravity-defying sculptures. It made Tim think of the cartoon landscapes of the road-runner show. His father leaned inside and poked the wall with his hand. A dusty cascade of milo came down, leaving another intricate wall in its place.

"Dirty, moldy stuff," he muttered. He walked to the truck, took the scoop shovel that hung on the tailgate, and handed it to Tim. "You got to poke it so's it goes down to feed the auger."

When the load was full, Tim shut off the auger and drove the heavy truck to the scale that stretched in front of the grain elevator office like an abbreviated airstrip. He nodded to his father at the desk, moved the big levers of the Fairbanks scale, punched in the weight, and drove around to the main elevator so Wilmer could unload him and put the milo into boxcars bound for Omaha.

Wilmer took a handful as it poured from the tailgate and brought it to his nose. His thin, craggy face screwed up. "Some musty stuff, ain't it?"

"Yeah, Dad says it's getting buggy."

Wilmer grabbed for a shovel to clean out the corners of the truck. "How's your mom?"

"Better," Tim said. "She's doing better."

"Good." The shovel clanged against the corners. Before the next load, Tim ate his lunch in the office, lounging on the daybed while his father worked at his desk and listened to the noon market reports on the radio. Tim liked bologna, but Mrs. Booker made them with butter instead of mustard, which made him faintly sick. He never said anything, though. The memory of the

Boy Scouts Indian costume was too fresh in his mind, his father wadding it up and asking who did he think he was, giving her extra work to do. Mrs. Booker had gone around sullen-faced for days, muttering against his dad.

"Yeah, it sure is hot," Tim said between bites. "But the milo's going like blue thunder. Ought to knock off two bins this afternoon."

His father turned around in the swivel chair, pausing to hawk up and spit in the sack he kept next to the desk. "Let's just make sure we get the one emptied today, okay?"

As milo roared into the truck for the next load, Tim, on tip-toes, leaned inside the bin, poked with his shovel to keep the grain coming down to the auger. He liked doing a man's work, doing it the way his brother did before he went off to college. Somebody had to be there steady. Wilmer missed a lot of days because he was a drunk, and his father took mornings off to go to the hospital.

Tim always thought he'd be the elevator man of the family. He liked to look at the towering silver elevator with its slope-shouldered sides and peaked headhouse. He imagined it as the fortress of the lower half of Julian, locked in struggle with the hill, part of town and its guardian water tower. Early in the summer, when he'd overheard his dad talk to a farmer friend about selling the elevator, he'd waited until they were alone and then tried to say that he could take care of things now and then by himself, but his father had cut him off with a short laugh.

The auger started clanking again, and Tim couldn't reach far enough in to get the grain down. Again his father came running, and Tim cringed in the accusing silence when the auger shut off.

His dad said, "You don't know nothing, damn kid." He yanked the shovel from Tim's hand, reached in the bin, and brought more grain down to the auger. He turned the juice back on and yelled above the racket, "You got to climb in there and knock it down. But not too much at a time so's it buries you."

Tim stepped into his father's cupped hands, and was boosted through the opening. He sank to his knees in the sea of tiny kernels. He stabbed gingerly at the wall, bringing down a great dusty waterfall of grain. He waited for it to go down, then collapsed more of the stuck milo. He found that he had to move constantly forward, as if on a treadmill, to keep his feet from drifting down to the whirling teeth of the auger. He dislodged a landslide that buried him to the waist, and it took all his strength to work himself free. With each fall of grain more dust filled the air, and it became difficult to see the upper rim of the grain. The bin was a dark dusty oven, and Tim felt his damp shirt grow heavy with clinging dust. Another cascade, and a thick dark blur flew past his ear, startling him. He turned quickly, in time to see the silhouette of a rat dive into the daylight. His gaze lingered there, finally fastening on the truck, which had milo overflowing on the cab and pouring onto the ground. He scrambled out of the bin, cranked the starter and jerked the truck ahead, with milo showering over the windshield. With the auger off, he cleaned up as much of the spill as he could, thankful that his father hadn't seen it.

Tim brought the truck to the scale and entered the office, covered head to toe with dust. He walked past his father and grabbed the dipper to the water bucket.

"Hey!" said his father. "You're getting milo dirt in the drinkwater. Don't you know nothing? Go dump it out and get us a fresh pail."

Tim looked at the thin film of dust on the water.

Protest welled up within him. His father didn't know how hard he worked to move that smelly milo. He yanked the bucket from the shelf and stalked outside to dump it. He went to the well, hung the bucket on the spout, and pumped the long iron handle. Halfway back to the office his pant leg brushed the rim and the water was contaminated again. He emptied and refilled again, and carried the heavy bucket painstakingly back to the office. Did his father expect him not to have a drink of water between loads when he was working in that tin furnace? He placed the bucket back on the shelf, faced his father, and blurted, "Well, how am I supposed to get a lousy drink then?"

His father slowly took off the dime-store bifocals he wore at the desk and looked at Tim. "Drink out of the pump, dummy. And don't let that auger wind out. I can hear it from in here."

Tim parked the truck beneath the auger, then climbed in the bin and scooped a big pile over the auger's mouth. He got out to turn on the machine, and was dismayed to see how quickly it sucked up his work. The slope of grain was no longer steep. He needed to use the shovel more and more to pull it downhill to the auger. Soon he was scooping nonstop. He coughed in the thick dust, the sharp intakes bringing more dust down his throat. Every time he stopped to catch his breath the auger rattled loudly, demandingly, and he could picture the dark look on his father's face. So he scooped, breathing the dust and feeling the layer of black sludge thicken on his clothes and skin.

He didn't bother to fill the back end of the truck. He weighed it and drove into the elevator, where Wilmer gave a low whistle at the sight of him.

"Drink?" Wilmer extended a half-finished bottle of Coke. Tim tasted the grit in his teeth as he drank.

"Go on, finish it. Just makes me wish it was beer anyways." Wilmer grinned, showing his bad teeth, and pulled something from his pocket. "Look here, Tim, an Indian-head nickel. You'll want to keep that for your coin collection."

Tim took it with a weak smile. "Thanks."

Wilmer turned to open the tailgate. "Filthy, dirty stuff ain't fit for man nor beast. Tell you what, Tim. You tell your dad you need a break. I'll take care of the next load. I can finish that boxcar in the morning."

When Tim brought the truck around, Wilmer was waiting by the bin, but Tim, climbing down from the cab, shook his head. "Dad says he promised that boxcar to Cargill tonight. I got to do the load myself."

"Your dad's crazy, Tim." Wilmer started toward the elevator. "You shouldn't be here at all, terrible time like this. You should be home."

Tim watched the back of his hands as he scooped. The sweat ran in his eyes, stinging them, but he had nothing to wipe them with. He found that if he stared at the back of his hands he could keep his eyes in a squint where he didn't have to scratch at them. The hands seemed to take on a life of their own—right on the handle, left on the shaft—as they guided the wide scoop back and forth through the swimming underworld of grain. The noise and heat made him lightheaded. He staggered through the grain, pushing scoopfuls to the auger, till at last he looked out and saw the mound of grain climbing above the side of the truck. He clambered out, turned off the auger and sat on the step of the truck, panting and dizzy. He noticed a stinging in his hands, and was surprised to see dirty pink rings of exploded blisters on his palms.

"What are you waiting for, first frost?"

"Have to move the truck," Tim answered, climbing quickly behind the wheel so his father would not see the tears gathering in his eyes. The auger rumbled to life before he was out of the truck, and Tim scrambled to get in and start scooping. The piles of grain were waist-high, and every bit that went to the auger had to be scooped. He pushed the grain to the machine faster and faster, barely keeping up. He coughed and choked, and his hands were on fire. Wilmer's voice echoed in his head. *Your dad's crazy . . . shouldn't be here . . . terrible time.* It came as a shock to realize Wilmer wasn't talking about the milo bin at all. *You should be home.* He could hardly stand being at home when he was there. Wild thoughts raced through his mind. He would hit his dad with the shovel, and he'd run away. He'd take the grain truck and get on the state highway and just keep driving and never come back.

From the back of the bin he thought he saw his father in the doorway, but he couldn't be sure in the brown particulate haze. "Turn if off! Stop it! Stop it!" But his voice was lost in the roar of the auger, and Tim kept scooping.

Finally it stopped. The quiet rang like thunder in his ears as he dragged himself to the door. His father opened the two lower doors and he stumbled through, dropping his shovel in the strange sunlight. Everything was too bright, too crisp, and shimmered at the edges. He held one nostril closed and blew black stringy slime from the other. He coughed, choking on the gobs of black mucus that rolled up from his throat and lungs. He began to panic, retching and grasping for air. A hand held his shoulder and another pounded his back. The retching turned to sobs, and the tears made vertical streaks on his coal miner's face.

"Catch your breath," his father said. "I'll unload. Go get a drink."

Tim walked to the pump, dizzy, sniffling, and coughing. His head pounded from the crying, but he couldn't make himself stop. He pumped the handle and splashed cold water on his face, his head, his shoulders. He put his mouth on the spout, drinking gallons, coughing and choking. "I ain't going back in there," he said to himself. "I don't care if he whips me dead, I ain't going in there again."

He stood by the pump a long time and finally wandered toward the office. He would stand up to his father. He would. He wasn't going back in there. He'd stand quiet and brave and take whatever his father wanted to dish out.

A green car was parked next to the scale. Tim sniffled back his tears as he saw a farm couple, James and Eva Swail, standing inside. They were dressed in city clothes. "Well, Harry," Eva was saying to his dad, "if you don't want to send a trifecta, I guess you'll just miss out. I seen in the paper one of them been paid four hundred dollars." Seeing Tim she laughed and said, "And aren't you a sight? You know, my boys would give anything to get that dirty. You be careful when you play around by the machinery, you hear?"

"I work here," Tim said stiffly.

"Oh, isn't that nice. Well, we're off to Omaha." She paused at the door. "Oh, how is Virginia?"

"Still bedridden," said Tim's father.

"Well, I don't blame her. I'd like to be bedridden myself for a few days to get me out of housework."

Tim's father hawked. He spat in his sack and took one slow step toward the lady. "The cancer's come back," he said quietly, in a voice that frightened Tim. "She's going in for another operation next week, but they don't know if they can do anything. Good enough excuse to get out of housework, you think?" He walked out, slamming the door.

"Well how was I to know?" Eva asked shrilly to the air. She turned to Tim. "When are they doing it? Are they taking her to Omaha again?"

Tim was powerless to speak or move.

James Swail took his wife's elbow, "Come on."

"What? What did I do?" Tim could still hear her as they shuffled across the scale and got in their car. "Not my fault she's dying or whatever. I was just asking."

As Tim walked out to the south bins, he saw Vaughn Jones wheeling the oxygen tank along the gravel street. His old eyes had a devilish gleam as he waved his mail toward the milo bin, where the auger rumbled and dust rolled out of the open door and drifted in the air. "Getting down to the dirty work now, boy," he wheezed, and continued down the road.

Tim found his shovel leaning against the bin. His father was inside the bin with a shovel of his own. As Tim hesitated, a pair of brown work gloves landed at his feet. "Those might help some," came the shout over the auger's roar.

Tim put on the gloves and stepped into the hot dark bin. Father and son bent their backs in the dust and scooped grain. Their feet sank to solid floor, and the bin echoed with the sound of shovels scraping concrete. Tim didn't know who he hated more, his father, old Vaughn, or Eva Swail. For months he had said, mechanically, when anybody asked, that she was doing better, and believed it was true. After all, his mom didn't come near the elevator, never worked in grain dust. It didn't make sense that she wasn't getting better. *Getting down to the dirty work now, boy.*

His father worked with closed mouth, methodically sliding the scoop from pile to auger, pile to auger, never lifting, always sliding. After a time, they turned off the auger. Together they wheeled the machine in, so that its mouth sat at the center of the bin. Tim repositioned the truck, and they began again. They shoveled the last piles to the auger and scraped inward from the walls, using the shovels like brooms. They poured the last scoopfuls down onto the auger's rotating tip, and they shut it off.

They stood on the dusty grass together, blowing brown slime from their noses and hawking it up from their throats. It wasn't spit, but a continuous rope of mucus, and every time you chewed a piece off to spit out, you found yourself gagging on more. As Tim recovered, he became more aware of the violence of his father's pain. He was all bent over, holding his sides, trying to blast air through thirty years of dust. Tim half expected to see blood on the grass.

Finally, his father began to breathe more like normal. He hawked a couple more times, then leaned and picked up his hat from where it had fallen when he was doubled over. He swatted it against his thigh, adjusted it on his head, and used thumb and forefinger to wipe the water from his eyes. He noticed Tim looking at him and gave a hard smile. "So you want to be an elevator man," he said. "Let's get to it then. We got two more bins to empty by Friday.

The Flowers

■ ■ ■

Alice Walker

It seemed to Myop as she skipped lightly from hen house to pigpen to smokehouse that the days had never been as beautiful as these. The air held a keenness that made her nose twitch. The harvesting of the corn and cotton, peanuts and squash, made each day a golden surprise that caused excited little tremors to run up her jaws.

Myop carried a short, knobby stick. She struck out at random at chickens she liked, and worked out the beat of a song on the fence around the pigpen. She felt light and good in the warm sun. She was ten, and nothing existed for her but her song, the stick clutched in her dark brown hand, and the tat-de-ta-ta-ta of accompaniment.

Turning her back on the rusty boards of her family's sharecropper cabin, Myop walked along the fence till it ran into the stream made by the spring. Around the spring, where the family got drinking water, silver ferns and wildflowers grew. Along the shallow banks pigs rooted. Myop watched the tiny white bubbles disrupt the thin black scale of soil and the water that silently rose and slid away down the stream.

She had explored the woods behind the house many times. Often, in late autumn, her mother took her to gather nuts among the fallen leaves. Today she made her own path, bouncing this way and that way, vaguely keeping an eye out for snakes. She found, in addition to various common but pretty ferns and leaves, an armful of strange blue flowers with velvety ridges and a sweet-suds bush full of the brown, fragrant buds.

By twelve o'clock, her arms laden with sprigs of her findings, she was a mile or more from home. She had often been as far before, but the strangeness of the land made it not as pleasant as her usual haunts. It seemed gloomy in the little cove in which she found herself. The air was damp, the silence close and deep.

Myop began to circle back to the house, back to the peacefulness of the morning. It was then she stepped smack into his eyes. Her heel became lodged in the broken ridge between brow and nose, and she reached down quickly, unafraid, to free herself. It was only when she saw his naked grin that she gave a little yelp of surprise.

He had been a tall man. From feet to neck covered a long space. His head lay beside him. When she pushed back the leaves and layers of earth and debris Myop saw that he'd had large white teeth, all of them cracked or broken, long fingers, and very big bones. All his clothes had rotted away except some threads of blue denim from his blue overalls. The buckles of the overalls had turned green.

Myop gazed around the spot with interest. Very near where she'd stepped into the head was a wild pink rose. As she picked it to add to her bundle she noticed a raised mound, a ring, around the rose's root. It was the rotted remains of a noose, a bit of shredding plowline, now blending benignly into the soil. Around an overhanging limb of a great spreading oak clung another piece. Frayed, rotted, bleached, and frazzled—barely there—but spinning restlessly in the breeze. Myop laid down her flowers.

And the summer was over.

What Happened During the Ice Storm

■ ■ ■

Jim Heynen

One winter there was a freezing rain. How beautiful! people said when things outside started to shine with ice. But the freezing rain kept coming. Tree branches glistened like glass. Then broke like glass. Ice thickened on the windows until everything outside blurred. Farmers moved their livesftock into the barns, and most animals were safe. But not the pheasants. Their eyes froze shut.

Some farmers went ice-skating down the gravel roads with clubs to harvest pheasants that sat helplessly in the roadside ditches. The boys went out into the freezing rain to find pheasants too. They saw dark spots along a fence. Pheasants, all right. Five or six of them. The boys slid their feet along slowly, trying not to break the ice that covered the snow. They slid up close to the pheasants. The pheasants pulled their heads down between their wings. They couldn't tell how easy it was to see them huddled there.

The boys stood still in the icy rain. Their breath came out in slow puffs of steam. The pheasants' breath came out in quick little white puffs. One lifted its head and turned it from side to side, but the pheasant was blindfolded with ice and didn't flush.

The boys had not brought clubs, or sacks, or anything but themselves. They stood over the pheasants, turning their own heads, looking at each other, each expecting the other to do something. To pounce on a pheasant, or to yell Bang! Things around them were shining and dripping with icy rain. The barbed-wire fence. The fence posts. The broken stems of grass. Even the grass seeds. The grass seeds looked like little yolks inside gelatin whites. And the pheasants looked like unborn birds glazed in egg white. Ice was hardening on the boy's caps and coats. Soon they would be covered with ice too.

Then one of the boys said, Shh. He was taking off his coat, the thin layer of ice splintering in flakes as he pulled his arms from the sleeves. But the inside of the coat was dry and warm. He covered two of the crouching pheasants with his coat, rounding the back of it over them like shell. The other boys did the same. They covered all the helpless pheasants. The small gray hens and the larger brown cocks. Now the boys felt the rain soaking through their shirts and freezing. They ran across the slippery fields, unsure of their footing, the ice clinging to their skin as they made their way toward the blurry lights of the house.

Who Had Good Ears

■ ■ ■

Jim Heynen

This boy had such good ears that he heard sounds others did not hear. Many of the sounds were bad sounds, like the squealing of a piglet that had been stepped on by its mother or the moaning of electrical motors drying the corn. Even the buzzing hum of fluorescent yard lights caught his ear, keeping him awake, grating on his nerves. Bad sounds made him jittery and made him a bad listener when grown-ups told him to settle down. After hearing so many other bad sounds, the grown-up voices came across to him like so much static on a poor radio channel.

But the boy with good ears also heard sweet sounds, like the breeze in the box elder tree outside his bedroom or the tiny waterfall sounds of the drainage tile emptying into the creek. While others heard the train whistle, he heard the musical clicking of the wheels on rail joints. He heard the path of silence left behind the train. He heard the weeds lean from the whoosh of air. He heard the ripple in a stream. He heard little symphonies in the ice-bound twigs rattling in the wind. But mostly what the boy heard were the songs of birds. While others heard airplanes overhead, he heard the meadowlark far in the distance. When others heard traffic on the gravel road, he heard pigeons in the barn eaves. The good sounds of birds were a warm bath to him, calming him down and making him a good listener when grown-ups told him what to do.

Because bird songs were his favorite sounds, he spent hours listening to them. Alone and silent behind bushes or fences, he was their best audience. But the day came when listening was not enough, and he started answering the birds as best he could. He started at night when only the owl was singing. Hooting like an owl was as easy as playing a penny whistle, and the owl responded by answering back. During the day, he went on to the more difficult songs of other birds, and what he found with the owl was true with the other birds too: when he answered them, they answered back. To him, their answers sounded like applause.

Not all bird songs were easy, he soon learned, but he practiced long and hard. Everyone told him he was good at bird songs. The birds seemed to agree. They were a kind audience, sometimes fluttering by to get a closer look at him when he was finished with his little concerts.

Encouraged by his success, he expanded his repertoire. Crow sounds he mastered in a day, though his good ears had some trouble telling him that either the crow's or his own cawing fell in the good sound category. In less than a week he had the blue jay down. The staccato chirps of the sparrow came easy for him, as did the predictable repetitions of the chickadee. But then came the cheek- and lip-tightening demands of the goldfinch and the air-swallowing gurgle of the pigeon. He went from bird to bird, changing the instruments of his fingers and lips and tongue to meet the challenge of each new audience. Sometimes a bird with high standards showed some signs of impatience with his imperfect renditions and, like a fussy choir director, repeated the song over and over in an effort to help him get it right.

Success at bird calling led to fantasies of larger audiences. Singing back to large flocks of ducks and geese seemed foolish, since he wanted to sound like a musician, not a hunter. He sought out huge flocks of starlings, but starlings lacked either patience or good taste and would flee at even his best imitations. He studied bird books and imagined traveling to exotic islands that were covered with colorful birds whose songs must be as varied and challenging as their colors. He was happy in his fantasies, but he had to live with the audience he could find on the farm.

He started roaming the fields, hoping to find every possible candidate: pheasants, quail, and what he could only think of as the little brown birds that fluttered in roadside ditches. Then, just when he felt he had exhausted both audience and repertoire, he had one terrible experience that changed everything. He had moved well beyond owl and crow, beyond sparrow and pigeon, beyond barn swallow and chickadee, and even beyond the complex riffs of the meadowlark and brown thrasher. But he made a mistake of wandering into the dark marshes of the red-winged blackbirds. He practiced for an entire mosquito-ridden afternoon and thought he had almost made an audience of the one he was imitating, when, with no warning, he was attacked from behind by a red-winged blackbird who lit into his hair like an eagle into a nest of field mice.

It was his first lesson in performing to an audience that did not like what it heard. Perhaps bored. Perhaps irritable. Perhaps threatened that he was upstaging them. He didn't stop making bird songs, but he could never put his fingers to his lips again without remembering that moment, no matter what his own good ears were telling him.

The Colt

■ ■ ■

Wallace Stegner

It was the swift coming of spring that let things happen. It was spring, and the opening of the roads, that took his father out of town. It was spring that clogged the river with floodwater and ice pans, sent the dogs racing in wild aimless packs, ripped the railroad bridge out and scattered it down the river for exuberant townspeople to fish out piecemeal. It was the spring that drove the whole town to the riverbank with pikepoles and coffeepots and boxes of sandwiches for an impromptu picnic, lifting their sober responsibilities out of them and making them whoop blessings on the Canadian Pacific Railway for a winter's firewood. Nothing might have gone wrong except for the coming of spring. Some of the neighbors might have noticed and let them know; Bruce might not have forgotten; his mother might have remembered and sent him out again after dark.

But the spring came, and the ice went out, and that night Bruce went to bed drunk and exhausted with excitement. In the restless sleep just before waking he dreamed of wolves and wild hunts, but when he awoke finally he realized that he had not been dreaming the noise. The window, wide open for the first time in months, let in a shivery draught of fresh, damp air, and he heard the faint yelping far down in the bend of the river.

He dressed and went downstairs, crowding his bottom into the warm oven, not because he was cold but because it had been a ritual for so long that not even the sight of the sun outside could convince him it wasn't necessary. The dogs were still yapping; he heard them through the open door.

"What's the matter with all the pooches?" he said. "Where's Spot?"

"He's out with them," his mother said. "They've probably got a porcupine treed. Dogs go crazy in the spring."

"It's dog days they go crazy."

"They go crazy in the spring, too." She hummed a little as she set the table. "You'd better go feed the horses. Breakfast won't be for ten minutes. And see if Daisy is all right."

Bruce stood perfectly still in the middle of the kitchen. "Oh my gosh!" he said. "I left Daisy picketed out all night!"

His mother's head jerked around. "Where?"

"Down in the bend."

"Where those dogs are?"

"Yes," he said, sick and afraid. "Maybe she's had her colt."

"She shouldn't for two or three days," his mother said. But just looking at her, he knew that it might be bad, that there was something to be afraid of. In another moment they were out the door, running.

But it couldn't be Daisy they were barking at, he thought as he raced around Chance's barn. He'd picketed her higher up, not clear down in the U where the dogs were. His eyes swept the brown, wet, close-cropped meadow, the edge of the brush where the river ran close under the north bench. The mare wasn't there! He opened his mouth and half turned, running, to shout at his mother coming behind him, and then sprinted for the deep curve of the bend.

As soon as he rounded the little clump of brush that fringed the outbank behind Chance's he saw them. The mare stood planted, a bay spot against the gray brush, and in front of her, on the ground, was another smaller spot. Six or eight dogs were leaping around, barking, sitting. Even at the distance he recognized Spot and the Chapmans' Airedale.

He shouted and pumped on. At a gravelly patch he stooped and clawed and straightened, still running, with a handful of pebbles. In one pausing, straddling, aiming motion he let fly a rock at the distant pack. It fell far short, but they turned their heads, sat on their haunches, and let out defiant short barks. Their tongues lolled as if they had run far.

Bruce yelled and threw again, one eye on the dogs and the other on the chestnut colt in front of the mare's feet. The mare's ears were back, and as he ran Bruce saw the colt's head bob up and down. It was all right then. The colt was alive. He slowed and came up quietly. Never move fast or speak loud around an animal, Pa said.

The colt struggled again, raised its head with white eyeballs rolling, spraddled its white-stockinged legs and tried to stand. "Easy, boy," Bruce said. "Take it easy, old fella." His mother arrived, getting her breath, her hair half down, and he turned to her gleefully. "It's all right, Ma. They didn't hurt anything. Isn't he a beauty, Ma?"

He stroked Daisy's nose. She was heaving, her ears pricking forward and back; her flanks were lathered, and she trembled. Patting her gently, he watched the colt, sitting now like a dog on its haunches, and his happiness that nothing had really been hurt bubbled out of him. "Lookit, Ma," he said. "He's got four white socks. Can I call him Socks, Ma? He sure is a nice colt, isn't he? Aren't you, Socks, old boy? " He reached down to touch the chestnut's forelock, and the colt struggled, pulling away.

Then Bruce saw his mother's face. It was quiet, too quiet. She hadn't answered a word at all to his jabber. Instead she knelt down, about ten feet from the squatting colt, and stared at it. The boy's eyes followed hers. There was something funny about . . .

"Ma!" he said. "What's the matter with its front feet?"

He left Daisy's head and came around, staring. The colt's pasterns looked bent—were bent, so that they flattened clear to the ground under its weight. Frightened by Bruce's movement, the chestnut flopped and floundered to its feet, pressing close to its mother. And it walked, Bruce saw, flat on its fetlocks, its hooves sticking out in front like a movie comedian's too-large shoes.

Bruce's mother pressed her lips together, shaking her head. She moved so gently that she got her hand on the colt's poll, and he bobbed against the pleasant scratching. "You poor broken-legged thing," she said with tears in her eyes. "You poor little friendly ruined thing!"

Still quietly, she turned toward the dogs, and for the first time in her life Bruce heard her curse. Quietly, almost in a whisper, she cursed them as they sat with hanging tongues just out of reach. "God damn you," she said. "God damn your wild hearts, chasing a mother and a poor little colt."

To Bruce, standing with trembling lip, she said, "Go

get Jim Enich. Tell him to bring a wagon. And don't cry. It's not your fault."

His mouth tightened, a sob jerked in his chest. He bit his lip and drew his face down tight to keep from crying, but his eyes filled and ran over.

"It is too my fault!" he said, and turned and ran.

Later, as they came in the wagon up along the cutbank, the colt tied down in the wagon box with his head sometimes lifting, sometimes bumping on the boards, the mare trotting after with chuckling vibrations of solicitude in her throat, Bruce leaned far over and tried to touch the colt's haunch. "Gee whiz!" he said. "Poor old Socks."

His mother's arm was around him, keeping him from leaning over too far. He didn't watch where they were until he heard his mother say in surprise and relief, "Why, there's Pa!"

Instantly he was terrified. He had forgotten and left Daisy staked out all night. It was his fault, the whole thing. He slid back into the seat and crouched between Enich and his mother, watching from that narrow space like a gopher from its hole. He saw the Ford against the barn and his father's big body leaning into it, pulling out gunny sacks and straw. There was mud all over the car, mud on his father's pants. He crouched deeper into his crevice and watched his father's face while his mother was telling what had happened.

Then Pa and Jim Enich lifted and slid the colt down to the ground, and Pa stopped to feel its fetlocks. His face was still, red from windburn, and his big square hands were muddy. After a long examination he straightened up.

"Would've been a nice colt, " he said. "Damn a pack of mangy mongrels, anyway." He brushed his pants and looked at Bruce's mother. "How come Daisy was out?"

"I told Bruce to take her out. The barn seems so cramped for her, and I thought it would do her good to stretch her legs. And then the ice went out, and the bridge with it, and there was a lot of excitement . . . " She spoke very fast, and in her voice Bruce heard the echo of his own fear and guilt. She was trying to protect him, but in his mind he knew he was to blame.

"I didn't mean to leave her out, Pa," he said. His voice squeaked, and he swallowed. "I was going to bring her in before supper, only when the bridge . . . "

His father's somber eyes rested on him, and he stopped. But his father didn't fly into a rage. He just seemed tired. He looked at the colt and then at Enich. "Total loss?" he said.

Enich had a leathery, withered face, with two deep creases from beside his nose to the corner of his mouth. A brown mole hid in the left one, and it emerged and disappeared as he chewed a dry grass stem. "Hide," he said.

Bruce closed his dry mouth, swallowed. "Pa!" he said. "It won't have to be shot, will it?"

"What else can you do with it?" his father said. "A crippled horse is no good. It's just plain mercy to shoot it."

"Give it to me, Pa. I'll keep it lying down and heal it up."

"Yeah," his father said, without sarcasm and without mirth. "You could keep it lying down about one hour."

Bruce's mother came up next to him, as if the two of them were standing against the others. "Jim," she said quickly, "isn't there some kind of brace you could put on it? I remember my dad had a horse that broke a leg below the knee, and he saved it that way."

"Not much chance, " Enich said. "Both legs, like that." He plucked a weed and stripped the dry branches from the stalk. "You can't make a horse understand he has to keep still."

"But wouldn't it be worth trying?" she said. "Children's bones heal so fast, I should think a colt's would too."

"I don't know. There's an outside chance, maybe."

"Bo," she said to her husband, "why don't we try it? It seems such a shame, a lovely colt like that."

"I know it's a shame!" he said. " I don't like shooting colts any better than you do. But I never saw a broken-legged colt get well. It'd just be a lot of worry and trouble, and then you'd have to shoot it finally anyway."

"Please," she said. She nodded at him slightly, and then the eyes of both were on Bruce. He felt the tears coming up again, and turned to grope for the colt's ears. It tried to struggle to its feet, and Enich put his foot on its neck. The mare chuckled anxiously.

"How much this hobble brace kind of thing cost?" the father said finally. Bruce turned again, his mouth open with hope.

"Two-three dollars, is all," Enich said.

"You think it's got a chance?"

"One in a thousand, maybe."

"All right. Let's go see MacDonald."

"Oh, good!" Bruce's mother said, and put her arm around him tight.

"I don't know whether it's good or not," the father said. "We might wish we never did it." To Bruce he said,

"It's your responsibility. You got to take complete care of it."

"I will!" Bruce said. He took his hand out of his pocket and rubbed below his eye with his knuckles. "I'll take care of it every day."

Big with contrition and shame and gratitude and the sudden sense of immense responsibility, he watched his father and Enich start for the house to get a tape measure. When they were thirty feet away he said loudly, "Thanks, Pa. Thanks an awful lot."

His father half turned, said something to Enich. Bruce stooped to stroke the colt, looked at his mother, started to laugh, and felt it turn horribly into a sob. When he turned away so that his mother wouldn't notice he saw his dog Spot looking inquiringly around the corner of the barn. Spot took three or four tentative steps and paused, wagging his tail. Very slowly (never speak loud or move fast around an animal) the boy bent and found a good-sized stone. He straightened casually, brought his arm back, and threw with all his might. The rock caught Spot squarely in the ribs. He yipped, tucked his tail, and scuttled around the barn, and Bruce chased him, throwing clods and stones and gravel, yelling, "Get out! Go on, get out of here or I'll kick you apart. Get out! Go on!"

So all that spring, while the world dried in the sun and the willows emerged from the floodwater and the mud left by the freshet hardened and caked among their roots, and the grass of the meadow greened and the river brush grew misty with tiny leaves and the dandelions spread yellow among the flats, Bruce tended his colt. While the other boys roamed the bench hills with .22's looking for gophers or rabbits or sage hens, he anxiously superintended the colt's nursing and watched it learn to nibble the grass. While his gang built a darkly secret hide-out in the deep brush beyond Hazard's, he was currying and brushing and trimming the chestnut mane. When packs of boys ran hare and hounds through the town and around the river's slow bends, he perched on the front porch with his slingshot and a can full of small round stones, waiting for stray dogs to appear. He waged a holy war on the dogs until they learned to detour widely around his house, and he never did completely forgive his own dog, Spot. His whole life was wrapped up in the hobbled, leg-ironed chestnut colt with the slow-motion lunging walk and the affectionate nibbling lips.

Every week or so Enich, who was now working out of town at the Half Diamond Bar, rode in and stopped. Always, with the expressionless quiet that was terrible to the boy, he stood and looked the colt over, bent to feel pastern and fetlock, stood back to watch the plunging walk when the boy held out a handful of grass. His expression said nothing; whatever he thought was hidden back of his leathery face as the dark mole was hidden in the crease beside his mouth. Bruce found himself watching that mole sometimes, as if revelation might lie there. But when he pressed Enich to tell him, when he said, "He's getting better, isn't he? He walks better, doesn't he, Mr. Enich? His ankles don't bend so much, do they?" the wrangler gave him little encouragement.

"Let him be awhile. He's growin', sure enough. Maybe give him another month."

May passed. The river was slow and clear again, and some of the boys were already swimming. School was almost over. And still Bruce paid attention to nothing but Socks. He willed so strongly that the colt should get well that he grew furious even at Daisy when she sometime wouldn't let the colt suck her as much as he wanted. He took a butcher knife and cut the long tender grass in the fence corners, where Socks cold not reach, and fed it to his pet by the handful. He trained him to nuzzle for sugar-lumps in his pockets. And back in his mind was a fear: in the middle of June they would be going to the homestead again, and if Socks weren't well by that time he might not be able to go.

"Pa," he said, a week before they planned to leave. "How much of a load are we going to have, going out to the homestead?"

"I don't know, wagonful, I suppose. Why?"

"I just wondered." He ran his fingers in a walking motion along the round edge of the dining table, and strayed into the other room. If they had a wagon load, then there was no way Socks could be loaded in and taken along. And he couldn't walk fifty miles. He'd get left behind before they got up on the bench, hobbling along like the little crippled boy in the Pied Piper, and they'd look back and see him trying to run, trying to keep up.

That picture was so painful that he cried over it in bed that night. But in the morning he dared to ask his father if they couldn't take Socks along to the farm. His father turned on him eyes as sober as Jim Enich's, and when he spoke it was with a kind of tired impatience. "How can he go? He couldn't walk it."

"But I want him to go, Pa!"

"Brucie," his mother said, "don't get your hopes up. You know we'd do it if we could, if it was possible."

"But, Ma . . . "

His father said, "What you want us to do, haul a broken-legged colt fifty miles?"

"He'd be well by the end of the summer, and he could walk back."

"Look," his father said. "Why can't you make up your mind to it? He isn't getting well. He isn't going to get well."

"He is too getting well!" Bruce shouted. He half stood up at the table, and his father looked at his mother and shrugged.

"Please, Bo," she said.

"Well, he's got to make up his mind to it sometime," he said.

Jim Enich's wagon pulled up on Saturday morning, and Bruce was out the door before his father could rise from his chair. "Hi, Mr. Enich," he said.

"Hello, Bub. How's your pony?"

"He's fine," Bruce said. "I think he's got a lot better since you saw him last."

"Uh-huh." Enich wrapped the lines around the whipstock and climbed down. "Tell me you're leaving next week."

"Yes," Bruce said. " Socks is in the back."

When they got into the back yard Bruce's father as there with his hands behind his back, studying the colt as it hobbled around. He looked at Enich. "What do you think?" he said. "The kid here thinks his colt can walk out to the homestead."

"Uh-huh," Enich said. "Well, I wouldn't say that." He inspected the chestnut, scratched between his ears. Socks bobbed, and snuffled at his pockets. "Kid's made quite a pet of him."

Bruce's father grunted. "That's just the damned trouble."

"I didn't think he could walk out," Bruce said. "I thought we could take him in the wagon, and then he'd be well enough to walk back in the fall."

"Uh," Enich said. "Let's take his braces off for a minute."

He unbuckled the triple straps on each leg, pulled the braces off, and stood back. The colt stood almost as flat on his fetlocks as he had the morning he was born. Even Bruce, watching with his whole mind tight and apprehensive, could see that. Enich shook his head.

"You see, Bruce?" his father said. "It's too bad, but he isn't getting better. You'll have to make up your mind . . . "

"He will get better, though!" Bruce said. "It just takes a long time, is all." He looked at his father's face, at Enich's, and neither one had any hope in it. But when Bruce opened his mouth to say something else his father's eyebrows drew down in sudden, unaccountable anger, and his hand made an impatient sawing motion in the air.

"We shouldn't have tried this in the first place," he said. "It just tangles everything up." He patted his coat pockets, felt in his vest. "Run in and get me a couple cigars."

Bruce hesitated, his eyes on Enich. "Run!" his father said harshly.

Reluctantly he released the colt's halter rope and started for the house. At the door he looked back, and his father and Enich were talking together, so low that their words didn't carry to where he stood. He saw his father shake his head, and Enich bend to pluck a grass stem. They were both against him, they both were sure Socks would never get well. Well, he would! There was some way.

He found the cigars, came out, and watched them both light up. Disappointment was a sickness in him, and mixed with disappointment was a question. When he could stand their silence no more he burst out with it. "But what are we going to *do*? He's got to have a place to stay."

"Look, kiddo." His father sat down on a sawhorse and took him by the arm. His face was serious and his voice gentle. "We can't take him out there. He isn't well enough to walk, and we can't haul him. So Jim here has offered to buy him. He'll give you three dollars for him, and when you come back, if you want, you might be able to buy him back. That is, if he's well. It'll be better to leave him with Jim."

"Well . . . " Bruce studied the mole on Enich's cheek. "Can you get him better by fall, Mr. Enich?"

"I wouldn't expect it, " Enich said. "He ain't got much of a show."

"If anybody can get him better, Jim can," his father said. "How's that deal sound to you?"

"Maybe when I come back he'll be all off his braces and running around like a horse afire," Bruce said. "Maybe next time I see him I can ride him." The mole disappeared as Enich tongued his cigar.

"Well, all right then," Bruce said, bothered by their stony-eyed silence. "But I sure hate to leave you behind, Socks, old boy."

"It's the best way all around," his father said. He talked fast, as if he were in a hurry. "Can you take him along now?"

"Oh, gee!" Bruce said. "Today?"

"Come on," his father said. "Let's get it over with."

Bruce stood by while they trussed the colt and hoisted him into the wagon box, and when Jim climbed in he cried out, "Hey, we forgot to put his hobbles back on." Jim and his father looked at each other.

His father shrugged. "All right," he said, and started putting the braces back on the trussed front legs.

"He might hurt himself if they weren't on," Bruce said. He leaned over the endgate stroking the white blazed face, and as the wagon pulled away he stood with tears in his eyes and the three dollars in his hand, watching the terrified straining of the colt's neck, the bony head raised above the endgate and the one white eye rolling.

Five days later, in the sun-slanting, dew-wet spring morning, they stood for the last time that summer on that front porch, the loaded wagon against the front fence. The father tossed the key in his hand and kicked the doorjamb. "Well, good-bye, Old Paint," he said. "See you in the fall."

As they went to the wagon Bruce sang loudly,

> *Good-bye, Old Paint, I'm leavin' Cheyenne,*
> *I'm leavin' Cheyenne, I'm goin' to Montana,*
> *Good-bye, Old Paint, I'm leavin' Cheyenne.*

"Turn it off," his father said. "You want to wake up the whole town?" He boosted Bruce into the back end, where he squirmed and wiggled his way neck-deep into the luggage. His mother, turning to see how he was settled, laughed at him. "You look like a baby owl in a nest," she said.

His father turned and winked at him. "Open your mouth and I'll drop in a mouse."

It was good to be leaving; the thought of the homestead was exciting. If he could have taken Socks along it would have been perfect, but he had to admit, looking around at the jammed wagon box, that there sure wasn't any room for him. He continued to sing softly as they rocked out into the road and turned east toward MacKenna's house, where they were leaving the keys.

At the low, sloughlike spot that had become the town's dump ground the road split, leaving the dump like an island in the middle. The boy sniffed at the old familiar smells of rust and tar-paper and ashes and refuse. He had collected a lot of old iron and tea lead and bottles and broken machinery and clocks, and once a perfectly good amberheaded cane, in that old dumpground. His father turned up the right fork, and as they passed the central part of the dump the wind, coming in from the northeast, brought a rotten, unbearable stench across them.

"Pee-you!" his mother said, and held her nose.

Bruce echoed her. "Pee-you! Pee-you-willy!" He clamped his nose shut and pretended to fall dead.

"Guess I better get to windward of that coming back," said his father.

They woke MacKenna up and left the key and started back. The things they passed were very sharp and clear to the boy. He was seeing them for the last time all summer. He noticed things he had never noticed so clearly before: how the hills came down into the river from the north like three folds in a blanket, how the stovepipe on the Chinaman's shack east of town had a little conical hat on it. He chanted at the things he saw.

"Good-bye, old Chinaman. Good-bye, old Frenchman River. Good-bye, old Dumpground, good-bye."

"Hold your noses," his father said. He eased the wagon into the other fork around the dump. "Somebody sure dumped something rotten."

He stared ahead, bending a little, and Bruce heard him swear. He slapped the reins on the team till they trotted. "What?" the mother said. Bruce, half rising to see what caused the speed, saw her lips go flat over her teeth, and a look on her face like the woman he had seen in the traveling dentist's chair, when the dentist dug a living nerve out of her tooth and then got down on his knees to hunt for it, and she sat there half raised in her seat, her face lifted.

"For gosh sakes," he said. And then he saw.

He screamed at them. "Ma, it's Socks! Stop, Pa! It's Socks!"

His father drove grimly ahead, not turning, not speaking, and his mother shook her head without looking around. He screamed again, but neither of them turned. And when he dug down into the load, burrowing in and shaking with long smothered sobs, they still said nothing.

So they left town, and as they wound up the dungway to the south bench there was not a word among them except his father's low, "For Christ sakes, I thought he was going to take it out of town." None of them looked back at the view they had always admired, the flat river bottom green with spring, its village snuggled in the loops of river. Bruce's eyes, pressed against the coats and blankets under him until his sight was a red haze, could still see through it the bloated, skinned body of the colt, the chestnut hair left a little way above the hooves, the iron braces still on the broken front legs.

Pick Up Your Pine

■ ■ ■

Kathleen Tyau

Aunty Hannah Mele got me the job in the pineapple cannery this summer. She got me the job because she has pull. Connections, pull, at least twenty years of pull—first as a packer, then as a trimmer, and now as forelady on one of the lines. Just tell the boss you're my niece, she said. Tell him you're fast. Tell him you're good.

Pineapple ripening red and gold in the field, pineapple waiting to be picked. Waiting for pickers to snap off their crowns. Crowns off and pineapples rolling onto the belts, into the trucks. Rolling, poking, and shoving with thorny skins, out of my way, out of my way. Pineapple ripe and rolling onto the belts, into the trucks, poking and shoving their way to the cannery in town, near the wharf.

I wait for the 5:30 bus in front of the mama-san, papa-san store down by the highway that goes into town. My jeans rustle as I pace in front of the store in the cool morning air. My jeans are stiff and very blue, and I have to roll up the cuffs four times. Even though it's still dark, papa-san has already opened the store. I long to buy something from the crackseed rack—a bag of cherry seed or red coconut balls. Something sweet to add to my lunch. My mother has packed me a bologna sandwich on brown Love's bread and a Red Delicious apple. But I haven't earned any money yet, and the bus pulls up, the inside lights still on. I sit in front, close to the driver. I press my face against the glass, watch for my stop, the building with the giant pineapple sitting on top.

Pineapple coming in from the fields, poking and shoving, and smelling ripe. The smell of ripe pineapple filling the air, falling thick and warm as a blanket. When the bus stops at the cannery, I can smell where I am.

Aunty Hannah Mele waves at me as I walk past her line. See you lunchtime, she says. She is one of my Hawaiian aunties, married to my goong goong's youngest brother. A tall, regal woman with long hair piled on her head like a crown. If not for the hairnet holding down her hair, I know it would glow. Girls, she says to the women sitting on stools, this is my niece Mahealani. Mahi, say hello. But these are not girls. Many of them are as old as she is, older than my mother, way older than me.

The whistle blows. Six-thirty. The boy feeds pine one by one to the genaka machine. The girls check him out. They shout, Oh da cute, but he cannot hear them. Oh da cute kine guy, our genaka boy is cuter than the others. Pineapple falling out of the genaka, pineapple rolling down the line, where the girls are shouting, where the girls are singing. Our pine is sweeter, our line is faster, the best in the whole cannery, no ka oi, no ka oi. Pineapple marching one by one down the line where the trimmers and packers wait. Pineapple with their cores removed and their skins chopped off. Pineapple already looking like cans.

I am a trimmer, and I will earn a nickel more than the packers. I'm not on Aunty Hannah Mele's line. I'm on my own and have my own forelady. She sees my red badge. Red instead of white, so she knows, so everybody knows, I am a child laborer, not yet sixteen.

Pineapples marching in front of me now. I sit at the front of the line, where the pine falls out of the genaka machine. Pick up your pine, pick up your pine, the forelady shouts, as the trimmers trim and the packers pack. The trimmers trim the eyes still staring from the pine, eyes that the genaka has missed, eyes that must not go in the cans. Roll the pineapple around on your thumb. Then make diagonal slashes across the pine with your knife. See the eyes fall out, four, five at a time. See how fast, that's what you want. No time to cut out one eye at a time. Then put the pineapple back on the line. Pick up your pine, pick up your pine.

You have to catch every one of the pine. Cut off the eyes before they get away. Cannot let even one slip by. So roll the pine faster on your thumb until your thumb muscle aches, and you see it swell and you see it grow and you wonder if your muscle will burst. Only half an hour has gone by and your thumb is already sore. One week sore, one month sore, sore and swelling, sore and aching, when will it stop? When will it stop?

The women next to me are singing, but I don't know the words. I can hear only the chopping of the genakas and the grinding of the belts and the clanking of the cans. And the forelady shouts from behind, Pick up your pine, pick up your pine. Other hands reach for the pine, but not mine. I am trying to spin a whole pineapple on my thumb. The forelady yells, paces up and down, finally yanks me from my stool at the front of the line and moves me to the end of the row of trimmers. She points at a plastic tub. She makes the words big in her mouth: Fill. It. Up. I remove pineapples from the belt that the trimmers have missed because they are one girl short, because of me. I grab the pineapples before they reach the slicing machine. Haul them to the front of the line where the faster trimmers trim. Eyes left and right flying off the pine. The girls are singing, knife blades flashing, and I am catching pine.

Pineapple twirling on thumbs, knives slashing, eyes falling into the trough, cans and belts clattering, banging. And the marching, pineapples marching down the line, from the trimmers to the slicing machine, from the slicer to the packers, from the packers to the cans. And all the way down the line, the forelady cries, Pick up your pine, pick up your pine.

The forelady pulls me from the line again. The whole line moves up a seat, including one of the packers. I move to the front of the line of packers. Next to the machine where the slices fall out. What about my extra nickel an hour? Are they going to pay me as a packer or a trimmer? A dollar quarter doesn't feel as good as a dollar thirty, but now I have to pick up only three or four slices of pine at a time. Neat, beautiful Life Saver slices, falling like fresh bread out of the bag. Looking even less like pineapples and more like cans now. Twelve or more slices at a time. Slices to admire, to toss into cans waiting on trays. Trays that the tray boys haul away.

But first you must decide. See the dark yellow slices, the translucent yellow, those are number one. All the rest are number two or three. If really bad, then number three, but try not to have number three. See the white flecks, the solid yellow. No flecks in number one, so this is two. Two not as sweet, but still good. Three is the worst, so you don't want three. Not as good money as one and two. Good lines have more number one. Number one is the best, no ka oi, no ka oi.

I stand at the best place in the line of packers. At the front, first in line, where I can scoop up all the number ones. I can pick up ones all day, smile, think how beautiful, how sweet the cans I've packed. Next time we go to the store I'll know how to look for the number-one cans. But the forelady yells at me, Pick up the rest! Pick them all up! The first four slices are easy, but not the ones that follow.

Pick up your pine, pick up your pine, the forelady shouts, and the trimmers trim and the packers pack and their lips mouth the words of the music trying to drown out the genaka machines. Knife blades flash to the beat, cans bang in the trays, and the pineapples march down the line, down the line.

Why have I never noticed ones and twos before? What if I put a two in a one can or a three in a two can? If a one goes in with a two, will they know? If a three becomes a two and a two becomes a one, then which is really a two, which is really a one? How do you know? How do you know?

The packer next to me on the line picks up all the slices I miss. She packs faster than I can think , and her cans fill up with number ones. Twos and threes evaporate. She sees what I cannot see fast enough. The forelady yanks me from where I am frozen, sticks me at the end of the line again, gives me a plastic tub. Points. I know. I pick up the slices the packer can't pack in time. Catch them before they fall into the trough and go where the trimmings go, to the juice, to the juice. To the juice, and what a waste of good pine.

Stop the line? Never happen. Never heard of such thing. Not this line, not my line. The forelady grabs the tub from me, and she and the first packer empty out the bin. Slices fly out of their hands and into the cans. Number one, number two. Number two, number three. Number one, so easy; number two, just like breathing.

Pick up your pine, pick up your pine, and don't get juice on your arms, don't get juice in your eyes. The juice can make your skin break. The juice can make your skin bleed, and you will have to go to the infirmary, and the nurse will wrap your arms in gauze, long strips of gauze, and everyone will know you were careless. Get juice in your eyes and she'll call an ambulance. The juice can make you blind. This is no joke, this is no joke.

A splash on my arm. A small squirt of juice. No, no, not me, but I show the forelady. Hold out my arm like it's diseased, not mine. She points to the infirmary, and the pine keeps rolling and the slices keep flying, and the nurse washes off my arm with lots and lots of soap and water. I don't see blood, I am lucky this time, but you can't take a chance. I stare at my arm, at the inch of raw skin turning pink, turning red. Is it the blood churning below? Is it the blood waiting to flow? Just one square inch of pink on my arm, and the nurse wraps my whole forearm in six inches of gauze. Six! All the way up to my elbow. Did you get any juice on the other one too? I shake my head no. But she checks, sees a little pink, wraps that one up too, just in case, just in case. But no juice in my eyes, so back to the line.

Back to the line, but I can't pack now. Can't pack, can't trim, too slow, can't get close to the pine with gauze on both arms, so the forelady makes me sweep. Set the broom, sweep the floor, let them see who you are. Let them see the gauze, see the badge. A red badge because still fifteen, a red badge and white gauze, gauze that hides blood. No more trimming and packing today for you. One arm wrapped in gauze is bad enough, but two. Two means you have to sweep the floor and everybody knows who you are.

The whistle blows. Eleven. Half an hour for lunch and only a half day gone. I spend ten minutes walking quickly to the locker room, taking off my gloves, washing my hands, using the toilet. I will need ten minutes to powder my hands and put the gloves back on. That leaves me ten minutes to eat. So walk fast to the cafeteria, where Aunty Hannah Mele sits. Waiting for me. She holds out a frosty can of guava juice. Oh, you got hurt, poor thing, but no worry, you will be okay, come and sit by me. You want a bite of my tuna fish? She gives me a piece of kulolo she has steamed the night before. She knows it's my favorite. She gives me some to eat now, some wrapped in foil to put in my locker and take home. I bite off chunks of the chewy taro pudding, savor the sweet taste of coconut milk.

After lunch the forelady sends me up the ladder. I climb way up, way above the packers and the trimmers, above the conveyor belts and genakas. I climb up the ladder and crawl across the catwalk over to the big chute. Everything that falls into the troughs passes through this chute. The pineapple pulp and the pineapple skin, the pineapple cores and the pineapple eyes, all the trimmings, all of it falling, falling out of the chute. Falling so fast I cannot see what is what. My job is to catch the knives, the knives that fall in the trough. The knives in this mess? The knives falling fast? But how can I see them? How can I catch them? Look for the blades, look for the shiny part of the knives. Catch them before they fall into the juice, before they jam up the machine and the whole cannery has to shut down, shut down. Grab them by the handle, not the blade, or you'll get cut and your fingers, your hands might fall into the juice, into the juice. Sit and watch everything falling, everything flying, and try not to think about what you heard at lunch about the boy whose arm got caught in the genaka machine. Where did the arm go? Into the trough? Into the chute? Did it get in the juice? Don't miss, don't catch the knife wrong or they will have to stop the lines and close the place down because of you. And who know what will happen to the juice, all of it turning red. Red, po ho, what a waste.

I catch two knives. Two, by the handle. Two very smart very fast good eyes saved the juice. Everything is falling, flying by, and I see it all and I do not see anything. I do not see what I am seeing, and my eyes are so tired, and I am so dizzy, and how did I catch them? How did the knives get up here? How did *I* get up here? I'm afraid I will fall into the pulp, fall into the juice. Where is the forelady, why doesn't she come? Everybody down there, working the line, will they forget about me up here? My head banging, my body shaking, and the whole cannery rushes by, rushes by.

The whistle blows. Three o'clock. Pau work. Silence except for rubber gloves snapping, feet shuffling, the girls saying goodbye. A kiss from Aunty Hannah Mele as I walk past her line. A kiss on my stink face. Don't worry about the arms. You'll be better tomorrow. So stink and the bus is already crowded and who wants to stand next to me. Not me. Stink and tired and hot and I want to sit down, lie down and go to sleep and never get up. Don't want to touch anybody. Don't want them to smell me, so hauna, so hauna. People get on the bus at every stop. They sit down, then stand up for anyone older than them. When one gets up and one sits down, all the people standing on the bus have to move to the back. Sit down, stand up, all the way home. I know they can smell the pineapple on me, on my clothes. Overripe pineapple, rotting in the sun. My jeans are no longer stiff, my cuffs unroll, shirt sticks to my back. The gauze itches my skin, and I want to scratch, scratch, scratch it all off.

Long walk up the hill in the afternoon sun. Take a bath, eat, fall into bed at eight. Pineapples still marching across the lawn, pineapples walking on the stone wall, fingers, legs falling into perfect slices on my plate. The forelady shouting, Pick up your pine, pick up your pine. I give up my seat on the bus to number one.

No pineapple in my fruit cocktail. This pineapple isn't ripe. Can't you see the yellow is wrong? No pineapple juice for me. Rub it with salt before you eat. No pineapple on my pizza. Wash your mouth, wash your hands before they bleed. No pineapple in my mai tai. No pina colada, please.

Aliceville

■ ■ ■

Tony Earley

We saw the geese from the road at dusk, a flock of maybe forty or fifty. They dropped suddenly out of the sky, miles from the nearest flyway, and landed in a bottom on one of our farms, just outside Aliceville, North Carolina. This was in December, on one of those still evenings in the new part of winter when you cannot decide whether it is a good thing to inhale deeply, the air is so clear and sharp.

Uncle Zeno and I were headed home—I don't remember now where we had been—and the geese came down on us like a revelation: a single gray and black goose shot from out of nowhere directly into the path of our truck, flying faster than you would imagine anything that big could fly. It was so low to the ground that we heard the whistle of its wings over the sound of the engine. And before we were even through jumping in our seats, the air around us exploded with honking geese, so close and flying so fast that they seemed in danger of crashing into the truck. Their rising shouts and the rushing sounds of their wings, coming on us so suddenly, were as loud and frightening as unexpected gunshots, and as strange to our ears as ancient tongues. Uncle Zeno slammed on the brakes so hard that the truck fishtailed in the gravel and left us crosswise in the road, facing the bottom.

The geese flew across the field and turned in a climbing curve against the wooded ridge on the other side of the creek back the way they had come, toward Uncle Zeno and me. They spread out their great wings, beating straight downward in short strokes, catching themselves in the air, and settled into the short corn stubble, probably a half mile from the road. And they disappeared then, in the middle of the field as we watched, through the distance and the dim winter light, as completely as if they had been ghosts. Uncle Zeno turned off the headlights, and then the engine, and we leaned forward and stared out into the growing darkness, until the ridge was black against the sky. Canada geese just did not on an ordinary day fly over the small place in which we lived our lives. We did not speak at first, and listened to our blood, and the winter silence around us, and wondered at the thing we had seen.

We decided on the way home, the sounds of flight still wild in our ears, that the geese bedded down in the bottom would be our secret, one that we would not share with Uncle Coran and Uncle Al, who were Uncle Zeno's brothers. My uncles were close, but they were competitive in the way that brothers often are—they could not fish or hunt without keeping score—and Uncle Zeno said that we could get a good one over on Uncle Coran and Uncle Al, who were twins, if we walked in at breakfast the next morning carrying a brace of Canadian geese. He hoped that we could sneak up on the flock just before dawn, while they were still bedded and cold, and thought that he could drop two, maybe three if he could reload fast enough, before they managed to get into the air and climb away from the bottom. He was as excited on the way home as I had ever seen him.

My mother was also to be excluded from our plans, because Uncle Zeno said that if she even looked at Uncle Coran and Uncle Al, they would know something was up, and would gang up on her until she told them our secret. My mother was fourteen years younger than Uncle Al and Uncle Coran, and twenty-one years younger than Uncle Zeno. They called her Sissy, and knew—even after she was a grandmother, and they were men of ancient and remarkable age—exactly what to say to make her mad enough to fight. It was impossible for her to lie to them about anything. We lived with Uncle Zeno on Depot Street, and Uncle Coran and Uncle Al lived on either side of us, in houses of their own. The five of us together ate as a family three times a day, at the long table in Uncle Zeno's dining room, meals that my mother cooked.

I managed to keep quiet about the geese during supper, although Uncle Coran and Uncle Al more than once commented on the possum-like nature of my grin. Uncle Zeno twice nudged me under the table with his foot, and narrowed his eyes in warning. The whole family knew something was up, and that Uncle Zeno was behind it. I enjoyed every minute of letting them know that I knew what it was. It was a position I was not often in. My mother slipped into my room that night after I went to bed, bearing in her apron a rare stick of peppermint. She broke it in two and presented me with half, which I accepted. We sucked on our candy in silence, staring at each other, until she asked, misjudging my allegiances, just what exactly Uncle Zeno and I were up to. I told her we were going to see a man about a dog, which is what Uncle Zeno would have said in reply to such a transparent attempt at bribery. My mother smiled—she always considered it a good sign to see parts of her brothers, particularly parts of Uncle Zeno, coming out in me—and told me to make sure that the dog would bark at a stranger, which was one of the many appropriate responses. After she kissed me and left the room, I heard Uncle Zeno in the kitchen loudly proclaiming that he didn't know what in the world they were talking about, that we weren't up to anything at all.

That night on their way back to their houses, Uncle Coran and Uncle Al stopped outside my window, pressed their faces against the glass, and growled like bears. I treated their performance with the disdain it deserved. I could not know then what the next day would bring, what Uncle Zeno and I would discover on our hunt. Most of the things that make you see the world and yourself in it differently, you do not imagine beforehand, and I suppose that is the best way. It enables us to live moment to moment in the things we hope to be true. I went to sleep that night possessor, along with my uncle, of what we thought to be a magnificent secret: in the morning a flock of Canadian geese would rise up before us into the air. They would be waiting, there in the frozen field, when we sneaked up on them in the new light.

In what seemed like only minutes, Uncle Zeno pulled my toe and held a finger to his lips. It was dark outside, for all I knew the deepest part of the night. I thought briefly about going back to sleep, into the dreams I had traveled through, and whose thresholds were still close by, but the thought of the geese exploding into the air, the secret adventure that I would share with Uncle Zeno, brought me fully awake. I kicked back the covers and gathered up my clothes and shoes and ran into the kitchen to dress beside the fire. Uncle Zeno was already wearing his hunting coat, and the legs of his overalls were stuffed down into the tall, black rubber boots he wore when he fed the stock. He was grinning. "Get a move on, Doc," he whispered, blowing on a cup of coffee. "Tonight me and you'll be eating a big old goose for dinner. You think we should let anybody else have any?" His shotgun was broken open and lying on the table. Neither his stock boots nor the gun, by my mother's decree, were supposed to be in the kitchen. I shook my head no. Let the rest of the world find their own geese.

When I was dressed, still shivering from my dash between sleep and the fire, Uncle Zeno and I started down the hall toward the darkness outside, and the things that waited for us in it, most of which we did not know. As we tiptoed past my mother's open door, she coughed, which stopped Uncle Zeno in his tracks. He shifted his gun to the other hand and dragged me by the collar back into the kitchen. From out of the straw basket that sat on the second shelf of the cupboard, he removed a piece of corn bread left over from supper the night before. "Here, Doc," he said, "you better eat this." He also poured me a glass of buttermilk. I gulped it all down. When we passed my mother's room a second time, we didn't hear a thing.

Once we made it out of the house, Uncle Zeno and I left in a hurry, pausing only long enough to scrape the ice off the windshield. If Uncle Al and Uncle Coran heard the sound of the truck starting in the yard, they did not dash barefoot out of their houses to see where we were going. And if our flight woke any of the hounds and pointers and assorted feists that divided their time and allegiances between our three houses, they did not crawl from out of their beds beneath the porches to investigate. We escaped cleanly, down the single block of Depot Street to the state highway.

Aliceville was still asleep as far as I could tell, the houses dark, and before Uncle Zeno even finished shifting into high gear we were out of the town completely and into the open country. There is a surveyor's iron stake driven into the ground underneath the depot that marks the exact center of Aliceville—I suppose that small boys still play games whose rules involve crawling through the spiderwebs and imagined snakes beneath the building to touch the stake, there at the center of things—and from that point the imaginary line marking the city limits is only a half mile away in any direction. Aliceville is a small but perfect circle on a map, and it sits in the middle of the fields that surround it like a small idea in danger of being forgotten. We lived our lives inside that circle, and made it a town by saying that it was.

The stars were still bright and close above us, but strange somehow, stopped at some private point in their spinning that I had never seen. The state highway was white in the beams of our headlights, and black beyond, and the expansion strips in the concrete bumped under our tires in the countable rhythm of distance passing. There was no sign yet of the coming day, although in the east, down close to the tops of the trees beyond the fields, there was a faint purple tint that disappeared if you stared at it very long and tried, in your wishing for light and warmth, to turn it into dawn. The fields beside the highway were white with a hard frost.

Two miles outside town, Uncle Zeno turned off the state highway onto the dirt road that ran past the bottom where the geese waited for us in the dark. He cut the headlights and slowed the truck to a stealthy crawl, the engine barely above idle. We crept along the road in the starlight until he stopped the truck and turned off the engine a mile or more away from the bottom, at the place where the creek that ran on the other side of it forded the road. "Don't slam the door, Doc," Uncle Zeno whispered. "From here on out, if we poot, they'll hear it. If we make a sound, we'll never see them."

Uncle Zeno loaded his double barrel with two shells out of his hunting coat, and gingerly clicked it shut. We were going to sneak up on the flock by walking in the creek, which had high banks and was hidden from view on both sides by thick underbrush. When we got close enough, we would run up out of the brush like Indians, and into the middle of the sleeping geese. They would explode into the frozen air around us for Uncle Zeno to shoot. I did not have any rubber boots, so I climbed onto Uncle Zeno's back—my uncles were tall, strong men who ran their last footrace down Depot Street on Uncle Zeno's sixtieth birthday—and I looped my arms around his neck and my legs around his waist. He shrugged once to get me higher on his back, and stepped over the thick mush ice that grew up out of the bank, and into the cold creek.

Uncle Zeno carried his gun in his right hand, and I felt its stock against my hip. We moved slowly downstream, and in a few steps the brush and trees that grew on the sides of the creek closed above our heads and hid us from whatever might have been watching. Uncle Zeno slid each foot in and out of the creek so quietly that I could not distinguish his steps from the noise made by the water.

We ducked beneath low-hanging vines and limbs and the trunks of trees that had fallen across the creek. I looked up through the thick branches and vines that were tangled above our heads, and could only occasionally see a star. They were dimmer, though it was still night, than when we had left home. I rested my chin on Uncle Zeno's shoulder and closed my eyes and listened to the sound of the creek moving by us in the dark. I might've even dozed off. When I opened my eyes I could sense the bottom on my left, its openness beneath the sky, but I could not see it yet through the laurel and briars. We were still a long way from the geese. Uncle Zeno tilted his head back until the stubble of his beard brushed my cheek, and he said "Shh" so softly that I almost couldn't hear it.

To this day, I do not know what sound we made that caused the geese to fly—how they knew we were there. We never saw them. We were still four or five hundred yards away when they took off, but I knew when it happened it was because of something we had done. We had been silly to think we could get close. When they rose from the bottom their wings pushing against the air sounded like a hard rain, one that might wake you up in the middle of the night. Their shouted cries were as exotic and urgent as they had been the night before, and I heard inside those cries frozen places we would never see. Uncle Zeno and I didn't move when they went up—we were so far away that it didn't startle us, but seemed inevitable somehow—and we stood still in the creek, with our heads cocked upward, listening. We could hear them a long time after they took off, spiraling upward in the sky, calling out, until they were high above us, almost out of earshot, and leaving our part of the world for good.

We listened to those last fading calls until even the possibility of hearing them again was gone, until not even our wishing could keep the familiar sounds we tried not to hear from returning into our lives. The creek moved around us as if we weren't there, along the edge of the bottom toward the river. A truck bound for New Carpenter on the state highway downshifted in the distance. A dog barked. I hid my face against Uncle Zeno's neck, suddenly ashamed of what we wanted to do, of the dark thing we had held in our hearts. At that moment I would have said a prayer to bring the geese back, to hide them again in the field, had I thought it would work. But I knew there was nothing I could do, no desperate bargain I could make, that it was over, just over. The simple presence of the geese had made our world seem less small, and we were smaller than we had been, once they were gone.

When Uncle Zeno finally moved, I was surprised to see that it was daylight. The trunks of the trees around us had changed from black to gray, as if the day had been waiting only for the geese to climb back into the sky. I could make out the faint red of the sand on the bottom of the creek, the dark green of the laurel on its banks. It was like waking up. Uncle Zeno let out a long breath and turned toward the bottom and waded out of the creek. I slid down onto the ground. "Well, Doc," he said, "I guess me and you might as well go on home." Through the undergrowth I saw the gray sky curving down toward the field. Somewhere a crow called out a warning. There was nothing remarkable about any of it, not that I could tell, not anymore.

Egg Boat

■ ■ ■

Nora Dauenhauer

In the fall of every year Qeixwnei and her family went trolling for coho salmon. The season for trolling usually opened mid-summer and the run became intense toward the end of the cannery season when the whole family went to the cannery to earn their money. Her father seined for the canning company while her Aunty Anny and sometimes her mother worked processing the catch from the salmon seiners. Because they worked for the cannery, they lived the summer season in the company houses.

Some years the catch of salmon seiners began to decrease before the seining season came to an end, but around this time coho trolling began to pick up. In order to get in on the favorable runs when the salmon began to migrate to the rivers for spawning, trollers had to be ready.

This was one of the times they were going to go fishing early. Her father had observed on their last trip that there were signs of coho, but he wasn't catching too much salmon in his seine. So he stripped his seine off the boat and began to replace it with trolling gear.

While Pop prepared the gas boat for trolling, the rest of the family packed their belongings from the company houses and transferred them to the boat. Everyone helped get everything aboard.

Mom packed things from their house while Grandma and Aunty packed things from theirs. Qeixwnei and her younger brothers and sisters carried things like pots and pans.

The old boys were big enough to help their father get the boat gassed up and get fresh water for the trip. So they had plenty to do, too, besides helping Grandma and Aunty pack their belongings down to the boat.

When the New Anny was finally ready, they left port in the early afternoon and headed toward Point Adolfus. The tide was going out, and they got on the right current which would carry them fast.

It was on a similar tide the previous year while they were coming to Hoonah from Cape Spencer that Qeixwnei's father spotted a little square-ended rowboat floating on the icy strait. He picked it up and he and the boys put it on the deck of the boat. They had it on deck when they stopped in Hoonah. Everyone saw it and commented on what a nice boat it was. Everyone noticed it wasn't one of the family's rowboats. When they arrived in Juneau, people noticed it too, but no one claimed it. There wasn't a fisherman who didn't know another fisherman or about another's boat, and no one knew whom the boat belonged to.

So Pop brought the boat up on the beach at their home at Marks Trail and started to work on it. He checked the boards to see if they were strong enough to hold the new materials he was going to apply to it and found that indeed they were strong enough and would hold them.

He began to renew it by stripping the old paint off. Then he caulked up the seams and finally put on some green paint left over from some other boat that had been painted before. He put a pair of oars in that didn't quite match. He tied an old piece of manila rope on the bow that could be used to tie it up with.

It was a good-looking boat. It looked just like the flower chalice of a skunk cabbage. And when he tried it, it had balance. It glided across the water very nicely. It was almost as wide as it was long. It was almost round and because it looked like an egg shell, they called it "Egg Boat."

Qeixwnei liked it very much and wanted to try it. She thought the boat was so cute. But when her father told her it was hers, she thought it was the most beautiful boat she had ever seen.

Her own boat! Why, she thought that it was going to be for one of her brothers. She could hardly believe the boat was hers. She was so happy she went around day-dreaming about it for the longest time.

Now she could go fishing on her own boat alongside her brothers, Aunty, and Grandma all by herself. It also meant she might catch a record-breaking salmon that she would fight for so long that she got exhausted from just the thought of it.

Or perhaps she and her Aunty and Grandma would hit a school of fish like she heard some fishing people talk about. She would fill up her little boat, empty it, then go back out and fill it again.

Or perhaps she would catch her the first king salmon, and she wouldn't care what size it was just as long as it was a king.

Her rowboat took her through many adventures during her day-dreaming. How exciting the next coho season was going to be. She was so happy.

■ ■ ■

And now they were actually going to the fishing ground. The boat moved along at a good speed. They all worked on their gear, giving it a last-minute check for weak spots and sections that needed replacements.

Mom steered the boat while Pop checked the tackle he would use on the big boat. She ran the boat a lot, taking over completely, especially when Pop had to do work on the deck or started catching a lot of salmon. Sometimes she even engineered. There was no pilot house control, so Pop would ring a bell to signal "slow," "fast," "neutral," "backwater," and so forth.

The boys were playing some kind of a game on deck. They said their gear was ready. Qeixwnei's Aunty wound her line onto her wooden fishing wheel. Grandma was taking a nap. She had been ready for quite some time. She was always ready for things.

As for Qeixwnei, she had her tackle that her Aunty had helped her get together from discarded gear left by various members of the family. She and her Aunty had made a line for her while she was still fishing in her Aunty's rowboat. Her spinner was the one her father had made for her the previous year from a discarded spoon. It was brass metal.

Her herring hook, however, was brand new. It was the one her Aunty had given her for her own. She was ready to fish, completely outfitted with the rubber boots her brother loaned her that were slightly too large.

She was so excited she could hardly eat. The family teased her that she was probably fasting for the record-breaking salmon.

When they finally got near enough to see the fishing ground, there were a lot of power boats trolling and others were anchored. A lot of the hand-trolling fleet was there too. Some of the hand trollers lived in tents out at Point Adolfus for the duration of the summer. When there were no salmon, the fishing people smoked halibut they jigged from the bay over past Point Adolfus. Some of the people were relatives of the family.

When they finally reached the fishing ground, everyone was anxious to get out and fish. They all took turns jumping into their boats while Pop and the two boys held the rowboats for them while the big boat was still moving along.

Grandma went first, then Aunty Anny, then at last Qeixwnei's turn came. The boys followed in the power skiff that was converted from a tender boat for seining.

They immediately began to troll. Grandma and Aunty Anny went close to the kelp beds along the shoreline. The boys stayed just on the outside of the kelp while Qeixwnei was all over the place and sometimes dragging the bottom.

She didn't even know where her father, mother, sister, and brothers were. She didn't notice a thing—just that she was going to catch her own salmon. Every time she dragged the bottom she was sure she had a strike.

Evening came and people began to go to their own ports. Grandma and Aunty waited for Qeixwnei for such a long time they thought she wasn't coming in for that night. When they finally got her to come along with them to go back to New Anny, it was near dark and uneasiness came on her. She had completely forgotten all about the kooshdaa qaa stories she had heard, where the Land Otter Man came and took people who were near drowning and kept them captive as one of them. She quickly pulled up her line and came along with her Grandma and Aunty Anny.

Everyone had caught salmon except Qeixwnei. It was so disappointing, especially when her brothers teased her about being skunked by saying, "Where's your big salmon, Qeixwnei? The rest of the family said she would probably catch one the next day and she shouldn't worry. She slept very little that night. Maybe she never ever was going to catch a salmon at all.

The next day the fish buyer who anchored his scow said that there were fish showing up at Home Shore and that he was going over there to buy fish on his tender.

Pop pulled up the anchor to start off for Home Shore. But halfway between Point Adolufs and Home Shore, the boat started to rock back and forth from a storm that had just started to blow. Chatham Strait was stuffed with dark clouds and rain. So they had to make a run for shelter instead of trolling that day—another disappointment for Qeixwnei, especially after standing on deck most of the way, straining her eyes to see if anyone was catching any salmon.

They holed up all night. She heard her father getting up from time to time during that night. He never slept much on nights of a storm.

Daybreak was beautiful. It was foggy, but through the fog they could see the sun was going to be very bright. Where the fog started to drop, the water surface was like a mirror except where the "spine of the tide"—the rip-tide—made ripples of tiny jumping waves on one side and on the other side had tiny tide navels. Sounds carried far. They could hear gulls, and a porpoise breathing somewhere, and splashing from fish jumps. It was going to be gorgeous.

They ate quickly and went off to the fishing ground.

Once again they took their turns getting into their boats while the big boat moved along.

This day Qeixwnei stuck really close to her Grandma and Aunty. They stayed on the tide spine, circling it as it moved along. She did everything they did. They measured fathoms by the span between their arms from fingertip to fingertip. Qeixwnei also measured her fathoms the same way. She checked her lines for kinks whenever one of them did theirs. She especially stayed close by when Aunty got her first strike of the day. She had hooked onto a lively one. Qeixwnei circled her and got as close as she dared without the salmon tangling their lines.

Then Grandma got her first salmon of the day.

Qeixwnei had just about given up hope of getting a salmon for that day when she got her strike. It was so strong that the strap that held onto the main line almost slipped from her hand. She grabbed for it just in time.

Splash! Out of the water jumped the salmon! At the same time—swish—the salmon took off with her line. The line made a scraping hum on the end of the boat where it was running out.

In the meantime the salmon jumped out into the air and made a gigantic splash. She could hear her Grandma saying, "My little grandchild! It might pull her overboard!" while her Aunty said, "Stay calm, stay calm, my little niece. Don't hold on too tight. Let it go when it runs."

Splash, splash, splash, splash, the salmon jumped with her line. It was going wild. It was a while before she could get it near enough to see that it was a coho and a good-sized one, too. She would get it close to the boat and then it would take off on the run again. Just when she had it close enough to hit with her gaffhook club, it would take off again. Several times she hit the water with the club instead of the fish because it kept wiggling out of range. Each time the salmon changed its direction the little boat did too, and the salmon pulled the little boat in every direction you could think of. The boat was like a little round dish, and the fish would make it spin.

At long last the salmon tired itself out, and when she pulled it to the boat it just sort of floated on top of the water. She clubbed it one good one. It had no fight left.

She dragged it aboard and everyone around her yelled for joy with her. Grandma and Aunty looked as if they had pulled in the fish. They both said, "Xwei! She's finally got it!" Qeixwnei was sopping wet. Her face was all beaded with water.

It was the only salmon she caught that day, but, by gosh, she brought it in herself. She sold the salmon and with some of the money she got for it she bought a pie for the family. What a feast that was! Everyone made pleasing comments about her so she could over-hear them.

They mainly wished she hadn't spent all her money on the pie and that she was going to start saving her fishing money for important things that a girl should have as she grew older.

It was great to be a troller. That fall was a very mem-orable one for Qeixwnei. Rain or shine she tried to rise with her Grandma and Aunty each dawn.

One day they all timed it just right for the salmon to feed. Everyone made good that day. There wasn't a fish-erman who wasn't happy about his or her catch that day. Qeixwnei also made good. When her Aunty and Grandma lined up their salmon on the beach for cleaning, she also had her eight salmon lined up. What a day that was!

When they got to Juneau after the season was over, everyone bought some of the things they'd said they would buy once the season was over. Pop bought some hot dogs for dinner and a watermelon that Grandma called "water berry."

Qeixwnei bought herself a pair of new hip boots. What dandies they were! They had red and white stripes all the way around the sole seams. And they also had patches that read "B. F. Goodrich" on each knee. And they fit perfectly if she wore two pairs of socks.

Her mother told her they were a very fine pair and that they would wear for a long time. Now she wouldn't have to borrow her brothers' boots anymore. In fact, they could borrow hers from time to time. And she could use the boots to play fishing with boats she and her brothers made from driftwood bark at Marks Trail. And very best of all—she would wear her boots when she went with her family to get fish for dryfish camp on their next trip.

The Raleigh Man

▪ ▪ ▪

Eric Gansworth

I passed Hoover The Dairy Man last Saturday on my way home from the grocery store. His red-and-white truck rumbled along the road. He stuck his arm out the open accordion door of his truck and waved as we went by. I think he knows just about everybody on the reservation. I raised my fingers a few inches off the steering wheel in response. He was making his Saturday run, which was shorter than his weekday deliveries. He delivered to only a few people on Saturdays, those who had been on his route since the time when the white scarecrow burnings were happening. That was about the time we lost The Raleigh Man.

The Raleigh Man used to come on Saturdays, too. They must have been Saturdays. Everybody was always around and it was the middle of the day. He must have come by all year round, but I remember him only in the summers. We'd all be playing in the mountain when we'd hear his weird horn.

His car horn wasn't like the usual kind. It didn't just honk. Instead, it played this little song. Years later, I heard these sorts of horns all over the place, mostly on customized vans and trucks with the monster tires. But back then, The Raleigh Man was the only one who had a horn like that.

As soon as we heard it, we always just left our plastic

Indian tribe in the mountain and ran to the big open space between my mom's house and my aunt's. That was where he always used to pull into.

I hadn't thought about The Raleigh Man in years. I saw Hoover just down the road from my family's plot of land, and as I stood in our driveway, and before I headed to my trailer, I stopped into my mom's house for a second. She was sitting on the couch doing some sewing.

"Hey, what did The Raleigh Man sell, anyway?" I asked. I couldn't really remember what his main goal in visiting us was.

"Oh jeez, lemme think," she said, setting her material down after poking the needle through it. "It seems like it was mostly cleaning stuff. Sponges, cleaners, scrub brushes, and some funny things, too. Spices, I remember this one time I was right in the middle of cooking some spaghetti, and I needed some oregano. Just then The Raleigh Man came pulling up like clockwork, and I sent Kay out to buy some from him.

"But I didn't have enough money for it, and when Kay came back and told me that, I was just gonna skip it. But then The Raleigh Man showed up at the door and said I could have it as long as he got to eat some of the spaghetti. I think that was the first time a white person was ever even in here. He even poured himself a drink from the water pail. He didn't seem to mind that we didn't have running water. What made you think of him?" she asked, smiling.

"Just thinking," I said and walked out the door. I was kind of baffled by that answer. I didn't remember any of that. I must not have cared too much about that kind of stuff. What I remember most about The Raleigh Man was the little red radio-controlled car and the cat masks. He kept these, with all of his other stuff, in the trunk of his car.

As he pulled up into the clearing, all of us kids crowded around his trunk. Even now, the smell of exhaust fumes weirdly excites me. The Raleigh Man always got slowly out of his car. He was a pretty old man to have this as his job. His skin was really pale, and his silvery hair was almost all gone on top. The few strands there always floated around in the breeze whenever he moved his head.

He wore a suit. I'm not sure, but it seemed as if it was always the same suit. Either that or he had a whole closet full of dark gray suits with pale yellow shirts. The suit was always kind of crumpled-looking. He brushed at it with his thin blue-veined hands as he got out of his car and walked slowly towards us. It never did any good, but he brushed away as if his hands were irons, magically straightening the material.

The Raleigh Man was something else. It wasn't that we never saw white people. We saw them at the store and places like that, and they sort of looked like The Raleigh Man, but we never talked to them. And the white people we did know didn't look anything like The Raleigh Man, at all.

They all lived in trailers. Most of them wore dirty white T-shirts that were stretched across huge beer bellies and work pants that didn't fit too well. They were always hiking their pants up, even if they were wearing belts. The bottom halves of their faces were always gray with stubble because they didn't shave too often. They also usually had these really nasty dogs tied up right near their trailers.

They had been living on the reservation since the

days when the state built the dike. They had come in to work on its construction, and after it was done, some of them must have liked living with us, because they stayed. But not everybody was too happy with this. The state had taken a big part of our living area, and now because of them, we had to share what we had left with those who had helped take the rest away. When we asked the state to get rid of their old workers, they told us they didn't have any jurisdiction out here.

We tried to discourage the old workers from living with us, asking them if they wouldn't like running water better. But a lot of them, when you asked them this, would simply crack another beer and say that pissing on the ground was just as easy as pissing in a bowl. So some people tried heckling them, I guess. They did things like driving cars in circles on the lawns where these men had settled, making big doughnuts in the grass.

With one particularly sickening guy, they shot out the transformer that kept his electricity connected. That seemed to work, and the guy left within the week. But this was not all that practical. When they shot out the transformer, about eight other houses lost their power, too. But people had gotten the right idea. We had to scare them off. Giving them hints wasn't working.

Someone got the idea to burn some dummies dressed up like the trailer guys. A lot of people went down to the "Dig-digs" to see if they could find some clothes that looked like the trailer guy's clothes. They found some old work pants and T-shirts, and Mel's mother, Vonnie, even donated one of her only good white sheets for the dummies' faces and hands, so no one would miss the point. They stuffed the bellies extra full and painted big red mouths on the faces.

They selected a clearing town down on Walmore for the burnings. That way they wouldn't have to worry about catching someone's field on fire. My mom wasn't planning on going. She was worried that the trailer guys might do something back and she didn't want us kids there. Then Kay offered to watch me if my mom really wanted to go down. She said okay, maybe just for a little while.

I really wanted to go, but my mom said that it might be too dangerous the first time, and besides, there were going to be plenty more. I'd have my chance after she checked it out. I complained, but she reminded me that I was only six, and that she could decide that I couldn't go to any burnings until I was grown up and could make the decision on my own. As she left, she also reminded me that it was Raleigh Man Day.

I went outside and sat on the porch, watching my mom as she drove out and headed toward Walmore. My cousin, Innis, from next door saw me and walked on over, to see if I wanted to go and play in the mountain. I shook my head, not interested. He said that he had some new ideas and this would be a good one, but I didn't take him up on it. He went to the mountain and brought the plastic tribe to our porch. We started playing and eventually we did move over to the mountain.

The hours disappeared as we gave our plastic Indians a whole new war to fight. Innis was right. We hadn't thought up this one before. He had boosted some Barbie doll Country Camper from the Dumpster at school. It had been in the girls' toy box, but the girls in his class totaled it and the teacher threw it away, deciding that it would be no good to anybody.

Innis had hidden from the bus when we were leaving to go home. He squatted in the group of kids after their teacher had counted heads, and then rolled into the shrubbery. He had to wait half an hour as his teacher got the room ready for Monday. But she finally left and he ran over to the Dumpster and crawled in. He found the Country Camper and walked home.

Innis brought the Country Camper home for his sister, Cynthia, but she didn't have a Barbie to go with it. The Camper became a fort for some of the Indians, and others attacked to try and get control of it. After one was counted dead, we set it aside, but only for a little while. Then it came back to life as someone else. There weren't too many Indians, so we had to bring the dead ones back to have enough people to fight.

When The Raleigh Man finally did show up, I almost didn't want to leave the battle, but Innis reminded me about the cat masks and the radio car. Maybe he'd drive the car this week.

He pulled up to his spot, and I ran into the house to tell Kay that The Raleigh Man was finally here. Kay's boyfriend, Peter, was in there with her. They weren't married, yet. They had just started seeing each other, so they were making out whenever they had the chance. I still have no idea how they met, since Peter was from another reservation a long ways away.

Wherever he did live, he came out to our res pretty often these days. They really did seem as if they were going to get married. I could especially tell when Kay said she didn't want to go see The Raleigh Man because she and Peter were busy. Her loss.

I ran back out and the trunk was already open. My Aunt Olive was there before me. Cynthia stayed in the house; she didn't like the cat masks. At first I thought that I must have taken longer than I thought, but then I noticed that Aunt Olive had her poncho folded over her arm. She was leaving for some place. She came and picked out a few things, paid for them with a couple of crumpled-up dollar bills that matched The Raleigh Man's suit, and sent Ace back to the house carrying these things.

Innis and I were trying on our cat masks. They came in different colors, but most of them were either blue or red. They looked just like a cat's face, right up to the muzzle. There was no chin on the mask. But it had whiskers on the top and bottom, and big cat ears, and eye holes shaped like cat eyes.

The masks were made of plastic and were shaped to fit kid's faces perfectly. They fit Innis and me, but not Ace. He had a really round face, and the masks always just sort of sat on his eyebrows for a few minutes before the cheap elastic that held the mask on broke. Ours always broke in a few days, too. The Raleigh Man kept a stack of them in his trunk. He knew that when he showed up the next week, these would be broken and lost, too.

So for Ace, he always kept something else. Once it was a balsa glider, and another time it was a parachute man. Ace always tried the mask on, anyway, in hopes that this week it wouldn't break. This week, of course, the mask broke as usual. But before Ace could even receive what The Raleigh Man had especially for him, Auntie Olive had sent him into the house with her supplies.

Innis and I were looking at the radio-controlled car in the trunk with our cat eyes when Auntie Olive turned to The Raleigh Man and told him it probably wasn't a good thing for him to be on the reservation that day. She advised him that he shouldn't make his usual stops and to just keep going.

She sounded pretty serious, so Innis whispered to me that it looked as if we weren't going to get to see the radio car this week. Occasionally, The Raleigh Man hooked the car up and drove it around in the clearing, hoping one day someone would buy it for us kids. No one ever did, but we still liked to see him drive it every once in a while. He hadn't done it at all that summer, so it seemed like the time was right, until Auntie Olive spoke.

She quickly walked away and got in her car and The Raleigh Man seemed to have gotten her message. He closed the trunk up and got in his car. He pulled out even before Ace could come back out of the house.

We went back to war in the mountain, but that didn't last long. Kay leaned out from the front screen door and yelled for me to come and get some shoes on. We were going somewhere. Peter was driving. Innis came running, too, but Kay said he couldn't come, this time. We were going down to the dummy burning, and she didn't want to be responsible for him.

Just before we left, I promised Innis that I would remember everything and tell him all the details. He said he'd try to make a little cloth dummy so we could act it out with our Indians once I got the scoop. I hopped in the car, and as we drove away, I watched Innis and Ace out the window. They were looking grim.

Peter was usually a nice guy. As we pulled out of the driveway, he said he was taking us to get ice cream before we went to the burning. We drove by the site and a lot of people were milling about. Some were in the trees stringing up the dummies, and others were on the ground admiring the stuffed figures and the handiwork skill in some of the stitching.

We didn't see any white people on the road, but we got kind of a strange look as we cruised by. As we were almost past, a solid, hard noise came from the back end, then another, and another. We were being bombed with dwarf green apples. I knew what they sounded like hitting cars. I had hit some before.

Peter slammed on the brakes and, throwing it into reverse, plowed his car into the clearing. A big group immediately surrounded us. Some people held on to boards with nails in them, and others had baseball bats. Peter jumped out of the car, swearing at whoever was closest, asking them if they were nuts.

They all looked at each other and then shifted, moving a little closer. Kay figured out what was going on and opened her door. Peter stuck his head in the window and told her to stay inside. She didn't listen. In fact, she grabbed me and dragged me out her door. She began shouting even before we were halfway out.

By the time we got out, a few inches were all that remained between Peter and the other men. Finally, someone recognized Kay and yelled to the guys that it was all right. They backed right off and Kay started yelling at some of them. They hadn't recognized Peter's car as belonging to any Indian they knew, so they bombed it. I went and stood with my mom and auntie.

Before Kay could get too far into her rant, we heard the sound of more apple bombs going off. The kids in the bushes had been instructed to bomb any car they didn't recognize, especially any new-looking car. The only people who had new cars on the reservation were the chiefs and they were already at the protest.

The car being bombed went off the road and almost landed in the ditch. It came to a stop and the bombing started again. Some of the men headed toward the road to see what the driver was going to do. I could see through the bushes that the car was maroon, the same color as The Raleigh Man's car.

I moved to another opening and could see the car's window. It was The Raleigh Man. I could see his old blue eyes, bugging out behind his old glasses, his forehead looking furrowed like a plowed field. They had to stop. Why were they going after The Raleigh Man? He never refused to leave, or anything.

I started shouting for them to stop. I figured that it worked for Kay, and I felt as if I had to do something for him. But before I had gotten more than a couple of words out, my mom had magically appeared next to me and whispered in my ear that I couldn't help him. He had to get out of this himself. Auntie Olive had warned him, but he didn't listen.

The Raleigh Man eventually recovered enough to get his car moving again, but by then it was dented all over the place. It was getting a little darker outside, and I couldn't see his blue eyes anymore. I had closed mine, anyway, and twitched every time another apple smashed into his car.

As the shadows grew thick and more people arrived, some of the men went to the trunks of their cars. I heard the latches and almost felt that Raleigh Man excitement, but I knew they didn't have any cat masks or radio-controlled cars. They pulled out some five-gallon gas cans and set them near the ghostly dummies.

A few guys scrambled back up the trees, and when they were steady, someone handed them the cans. They poured the gasoline on the dummies, and after they climbed down, everyone gathered around for the lighting. The dummies danced in the igniting flames, then twirled like ballerinas as they burned.

Most everyone seemed to be having a good time, but no one mentioned the trailer guys. They talked only about what good times they used to have before the state changed everything. I thought about the good times I wouldn't be having anymore. Though it's usually the state's fault, this time it really wasn't. With a few more burnings, we finally got rid of the trailer guys, but I didn't even care anymore.

When we got home, Innis asked me to tell him everything, but I wouldn't say anything. Someone else must have told him, though. He didn't seem too surprised when The Raleigh Man didn't come by the next week, or the next, or the next. But I never spoke of it. I didn't want anybody to look back on that day with fondness.

Golden Glass

■ ■ ■

Alma Villanueva

It was his fourteenth summer. He was thinning out, becoming angular and clumsy, but the cautiousness, the old-man seriousness he'd had as a baby, kept him contained, ageless and safe. His humor, always dry and to the bone since a small child, let you know he was watching everything.

He seemed always to be at the center of his own universe, so it was no surprise to his mother to hear Ted say: "I'm building a fort and sleeping out in it all summer, and I won't come in for anything, not even food. Okay?"

This had been their silent communion, the steady presence of love that flowed regularly, daily—food. The presence of his mother preparing it, his great appetite and obvious enjoyment of it—his nose smelling everything, seeing his mother more vividly than with his eyes.

He watched her now for signs of offense, alarm, and only saw interest. "Where will you put the fort?" Vida asked.

She trusted him to build well and not ruin things, but of course she had to know where. She looked at his dark, contained face and her eyes turned in and saw him when he was small, with curly golden hair, when he wrapped his arms around her neck. Their quiet times—

undemanding—he could be let down, and a small toy could delight him for hours. She thought of the year he began kissing her elbow in passing, the way he preferred. Vida would touch his hair, his forehead, his shoulders—the body breathing out at the touch, his stillness. Then the explosion out the door told her he needed her touch, still.

"I'll build it by the redwoods, in the cypress trees. Okay?"

"Make sure you keep your nails together and don't dig into the trees. I'll be checking. If the trees get damaged, it'll have to come down."

"Jason already said he'd bring my food and stuff."

"Where do you plan to shower and go to the bathroom?" Vida wondered.

"With the hose when it's hot and I'll dig holes behind the barn," Ted said so quietly as to seem unspoken. He knew how to slither under her, smoothly, like silk.

"Sounds interesting, but it better stay clean—this place isn't that big. Also, on your dinner night, you can cook outdoors."

His eyes flashed, but he said, "Okay."

He began to gather wood from various stacks, drying it patiently from the long rains. He kept in his room one of the hammers and a supply of nails that he'd brought. It was early June and the seasonal creek was still running. It was pretty dark out there and he wondered if he'd meant what he'd said.

Ted hadn't seen his father in nearly four years, and he didn't miss him like you should a regular father, he thought. His father's image blurred with the memory of a football hitting him too hard, pointed (a bullet), right in the stomach, and the punishment for the penny candies—a test his father had set up for him to fail. His stomach hardened at the thought of his father, and he found he didn't miss him at all.

He began to look at the shapes of the trees, where the limbs were solid, where a space was provided (he knew his mother really would make him tear down the fort if he hurt the trees). The cypress was right next to the redwoods, making it seem very remote. Redwoods do that— they suck up sound and time and smell like another place. So he counted the footsteps, when no one was looking, from the fort to the house. He couldn't believe it was so close; it seemed so separate, alone—especially in the dark, when the only safe way of travel seemed flight (invisible at best).

Ted had seen his mother walk out to the bridge at night with a glass of wine, looking into the water, listening to it. He knew she loved to see the moon's reflection in the water. She'd pointed it out to him once by a river where they camped, her face full of longing—too naked somehow, he thought. Then, she swam out into the water, at night, as though trying to touch the moon. He wouldn't look at her. He sat and glared at the fire and roasted another marshmallow the way he liked it: bubbly, soft, and brown (maybe six if he could get away with it). Then she'd be back, chilled and bright, and he was glad she went. Maybe I like the moon too, he thought, involuntarily, as though the thought weren't his own—but it was.

He build the ground floor directly on the earth, with a cover of old plywood, then scattered remnant rugs that he'd asked Vida to get for him. He concocted a latch and a door, with his hand ax over it, just in case. He brought his sleeping bag, some pillows, a transistor radio, some clothes, and moved in for the summer. The first week he slept with his buck knife open in his hand and his pellet gun loaded on the same side, his right. The second week Ted sheathed the knife and put it under his head, but kept the pellet gun loaded at all times. He missed no one in the house but the dog, so he brought him into the cramped little space, enduring dog breath and farts because he missed *someone*.

Ted thought of when his father left, when they lived in the city, with forty kids on one side of the block and forty on the other. He remembered that one little kid with the funny sores on his body who chose an apple over candy every time. He worried they would starve or something worse. That time he woke up screaming in his room (he forgot why), and his sister began crying at the same time, "Someone's in here," as though they were having the same terrible dream. Vida ran in with a chair in one hand and a kitchen knife in the other, which frightened them even more. But when their mother realized it was only their hysteria, she became angry and left. Later they all laughed about this till they cried, including Vida, and things felt safer.

He began to build the top floor now but he had to prune some limbs out of the way. Well, that was okay as long as he was careful. So he stacked them to one side for kindling and began to brace things in place. It felt weird going up into the tree, not as safe as his small, contained place on the ground. He began to build it, thinking of light. He could bring his comic books, new ones, sit up straight, and eat snacks in the daytime. He would put in a side window facing the house to watch them, if he wanted, and a tunnel from the bottom floor to the top. Also, a ladder he'd found and repaired—he could pull it up and place it on hooks, out of reach. A hatch at the top of the ceiling for leaving or entering, tied down inside with a rope. He began to sleep up here, without the dog, with the tunnel closed off.

Vida noticed Ted had become cheerful and would stand next to her, to her left side, talking sometimes. But she realized she mustn't face him or he'd become silent and wander away. So she stood listening, in the same even breath and heartbeat she kept when she spotted the wild pheasants with their long, lush tails trailing the grape arbor, picking delicately and greedily at the unpicked grapes in the early autumn light. So sharp, so perfect, so rare to see a wild thing at peace.

She knew he ate well—his brother brought out a half gallon of milk that never came back, waiting to be asked to join him, but never daring to ask. His sister made him an extra piece of ham for his four eggs; most always he ate cold cereal and fruit or got a hot chocolate on his way to summer school. They treated Ted somewhat like a stranger, because he was.

Ted was taking a makeup course and one in stained glass. There, he talked and acted relaxed, like a boy; no one expected any more or less. The colors of the stained glass were deep and beautiful, and special—you couldn't waste this glass. The sides were sharp, the cuts were slow and meticulous with a steady pressure. The design's plan had to be absolutely followed or the beautiful glass would go to waste, and he'd curse himself.

It was late August and Ted hadn't gone inside the house once. He liked waking up, hearing nothing but birds—not his mother's voice or his sister's or his brother's. He could tell the various bird calls and liked the soft brown quail call the best. He imagined their taste and wondered if their flesh was as soft as their song. Quail would've been okay to kill, as long as he ate it, his mother said. Instead, he killed jays because they irritated him so much with their shrill cries. Besides, a neighbor paid Ted per bird because he didn't want them in his garden. But that was last summer and he didn't do that anymore, and the quail were proud and plump and swift, and Ted was glad.

The stained glass was finished and he decided to place it in his fort facing the back fields. In fact, it looked like the back fields—trees and the sun in a dark sky. During the day the glass sun shimmered a beautiful yellow, the blue a much better color than the sky outside: deeper, like night.

He was so used to sleeping outside now he didn't wake up during the night, just like in the house. One night, toward the end when he'd have to move back with everyone (school was starting, frost was coming and the rains), Ted woke up to see the stained glass full of light. The little sun was a golden moon and the inside glass sky and the outside sky matched.

In a few days he'd be inside, and he wouldn't mind at all.

I Have the Serpent Brought

■ ■ ■

Vicky Wicks

And that this place may thoroughly be thought
True Paradise, I have the serpent brought.
 —*John Donne, "Twickenham Garden"*

In the south pasture the child sits on her favorite rock, the gray one with garnet crystals sparkling red in sunlight. She has always imagined the crystals to be red diamonds and has determined that someday she will get a hammer and chisel and bust those diamonds out of the rock and sell them for millions of dollars, but not today. Today she luxuriates in self-pity brought on by her father's rapping her on the head and telling her to get out of his hair, and she hopes that the magic from the crystals will course up her spine and soothe the ache in her throat. It is a day in late June, the last day of spring, and the sun burns through the child's thin cotton blouse, warming her back as she sits hunched over with her elbows on her knees and her chin resting in her hands.

The child's rock juts out from a pile of stones on the bank of a creek lined with trees, and the sparkling trickle of water sings while the wind makes the trees groan. Swaying wildflowers wave to catch the child's attention. She knows the names of some of these flowers—Queen Anne's lace and wild roses and black-eyed Susans—because she has picked them for her mother and her mother has introduced them to her. Late last summer she broke off a stalk of milkweed and, with white sticky sap oozing onto her hands, took it to her mother. Her mother explained that not so long ago, during World War II, she and her sister collected the pods so that the silk could be made into parachutes; the child then took the plant outside to tear open the pods and watch the parachute stuff carried away by the wind.

But today the milkweed stems bear no pods, only clusters of violet flowers, and they hold no interest for the child. She turns away from them, raises her face toward the sun, closes her eyes against white glare. The sun shines through her eyelids and for a short while she is enthralled by watching changing hues of red, awed by knowing that she is looking at her own blood. But a shadow flashes cool blue and she opens her eyes to watch for the hawk she knows is there; when she sees him, she wishes he could drop down, clutch her collar in his talons, and float her far away to never again. Her eyes burning now, she drops her gaze and finds the landscape whitewashed, indistinct. She stands and walks toward the creek, to a tree, to clear her vision in its cool shade, and then, near a mound in the pasture twenty yards south, she sees movement.

Shading her eyes with her hand, she sees what she believes to be two puppies chasing one another through the yellow grass. One tackles the other from behind and bites his ears, and the second pup rolls over to wrestle the one on top. The pups are brownish-red with black paws and white stomachs, and the child wants to touch them and hold them. Even better, she'll catch them and take them home with her. They will be her pets, owned solely by her, and her brothers will be sorry that they wouldn't let her play with them today because she's a girl, which is why she was bothering her father in the first place.

Staying behind trees along the riverbank, the child manages to creep a few yards closer to the pups, close enough to see their bushy tails and to realize that they are fox cubs, not puppies. This is better still—everybody has a dog but she will be the only one to have foxes.

She leaves the cover of the trees and hunches over, trying to make herself small, tiptoeing across open pasture closer to the cubs. Suddenly the girl freezes. The cubs have seen her and, after starting for a couple of heartbeats, have run to the top of the tiny hill to peer over it with round, shiny black eyes. The child and the cubs, all stock-still, exchange curious stares.

The girl backs away slowly, still hunched over, toward the trees. Her heart pounds in her chest, and she wonders if the cubs' hearts are pounding too. She reaches the shelter of a tree trunk, edges around to the side away from the cubs, and presses her back against the rough bark to hide her body. She waits. Before her the stream tumbles over smooth pebbles, still fed by spring rains, not yet dried up as it will be in August.

Above her in the branches a bird scolds. The girl peers around the tree trunk to see if the commotion keeps the foxes alert. It does. The cubs are still frozen at the top of the mound, staring in her direction. To catch them, she will need help. She looks to the north, where she can see the white farmhouse small with distance.

She moves slowly toward the creek and down its bank, her feet sliding on soft mud. Carefully she follows the creek bed, picking up clumps of mud and soaking her shoes when her feet slip off the bank and into the water. When she is sure she has gone far enough to be out of the cubs' sight, she scrambles up the bank to high, dry ground and then breaks into a run. The wind tears at her face, pulling her eyes back and tugging at her ponytail, and she can't hear anything through the roar of the wind but her own breath and the plodding thud of her muddy feet hitting the powder-soft dirt of the cowpath.

When she reaches the farmhouse, she tiptoes across the porch, past her old dog Buster snoozing in the shade, and opens and closes the screen door carefully, not letting it bang shut behind her. Her mother has gone into town and her brothers are outside somewhere, playing make-believe in a world of their own creation; the house breathes quietly and every creaking floorboard echoes in the child's ears.

In the living room on the couch, her father lies on his side, his knees bent, his head resting on his right bicep, his right forearm sticking straight up into the air, his hand curling down toward his face. He is snoring softly. His boots stand side by side on the floor, at ease but not off duty. The mantle clock on top of the upright piano loudly marks the passage of seconds with a thudding tock-tock-tock, and the child, not wanting her head smacked again, pulls herself carefully into the rocking chair to silently wait for her father to wake up. She tries to sit very still, knowing that the wood of the rocker will creak if she moves, but, as her dad has often noted, sitting still is not her high suit. She shifts her weight on the seat and the chair lets out a loud groan.

Her father also grunts and rolls onto his back. He opens his eyes and looks at the child, rubs his eyes with his thumb and forefinger, and asks hoarsely, "What you up to?"

"I'm just waitin' for you to wake up so I can tell you somethin'," she replies.

"What."

"You sure you're ready to wake up? 'Cuz I can wait if you ain't."

"That's okay," her father says. "I need to get started on chores anyway."

The child watches her father rise to a sitting position and determines that his nap has improved his mood, and so, in an excited stream of chatter, she tells him about the fox cubs in the south pasture and how she wants to capture them to be her pets.

Her father sits staring silently at her, and in his eyes is surprising tenderness. After a few moments, he speaks, softly.

"Katie, you know we been losing chickens."

The child sits back in the rocking chair and shrinks down in the seat, suddenly wishing she had just kept quiet.

"But these fox are just babies. It couldn't be them that's killing chickens."

"They'll kill chickens when they grow up."

"I won't let them. I'll take real good care of them and pet them and they'll grow up real nice and gentle and they wouldn't hurt a fly."

Her father sighs as he pulls on his boots and again when he gets up from the couch. The child struggles out of the rocking chair and stands also. She follows him as he walks through the kitchen to the entryway.

"You got mud on the floor," her father says as he takes his rifle from the closet.

"I'm sorry," she says, and she moves quickly to the closet to get the broom. Her father stops her.

"You can clean it up later," he says, again with that confusing tenderness. "I need you to show me where the fox are."

The child wants to tell him no, but she can't.

Outside, on the porch, the dog looks up at her father and then jumps up, his tail wagging. Her father reaches down to scratch the dog behind one ear. "Stay here, Buster," her father says. "There's a good dog."

As father and daughter walk side by side toward the south pasture, she tries to win the cubs a reprieve through promises: she'll never allow them to become killers. Her father continues to speak gently to her, but he is firm: killing is in their blood. The wind is at her back and she can hear his words clearly.

When the girl and her father reach the rock pile, they crouch behind it and watch the foxes who are again out of their den, wrestling in the field of grass.

"You better go on back to the house now," her father says softly. The girl shakes her head no. Her father looks intently at her for a few seconds. "Stay here, then," he says before he creeps away from her, following the tree line until he reaches a point directly east of the foxes. The girl watches her father drop to one knee and raise the rifle to his shoulder. The cubs, sensing danger, stop their free-for-all and sit, their ears sticking up, their black eyes turned toward her. The child jams her fingers in her ears and hears a dim and hollow pop. One of the cubs falls back and rolls. Another pop. The second cub, on the run, drops, tries to crawl. The third shot stops him.

The father stands and he and his daughter move toward the cubs, reaching them at the same time. The father kneels by the first fox he shot, and the child examines the body over his shoulder. She thinks she sees the pup moving and she hopes that it is still alive, but after a few seconds she sees that only its fur is moving, blown by the wind. She squats beside her father and looks at the cub's face. She now can see that its eyes are brown, not black; they are open and staring at something she can't see. Sticking out between the fox's tiny white teeth is the tip of its pink tongue. The animal looks as if it is frozen, but when the child reaches out to pet it, the fur feels warm and soft. Her throat is aching now just as it was earlier, before she saw the cubs playing on the yellow grass in the sunshine.

Her father is very still, kneeling beside the cub's body, and his head is lowered. She can't see his face but she hears his voice say, "Katie, you know it had to be done," and he wipes his eyes with his fingers before turning to look at her.

"I know," she says.

The child and her father walk to the body of the second cub to make sure it's not still alive and suffering. It is dead. It lies as still as its brother, and the father and daughter stand over its body, giving it silent respect.

The man then turns and says he can't wait for the mother fox to come back; it's time to milk the cows. He and his daughter walk together toward the house, the man walking through thick grass, the child on the cowpath. They are silent as they walk. The wind rumbles in her ears. She thinks about the mother fox and wonders if, like killing chickens, sorrow for her children is also in her blood. Tomorrow, the child vows silently, she will come back to the south pasture with a spade and dig a grave for the cubs so that wildflowers and prairie grass will cover them over. She looks up at her father and wants to ask if he will help, but she can't; her words drift away on the wind.

The Salamanders

■ ■ ■

Tomás Rivera

What I remember most about that night is the darkness, the mud and the slime of the salamanders. But I should start from the beginning so you can understand all of this, and how, upon feeling this, I understood something that I still have with me. But I don't have this with me only as something I remember, but as something that I still feel.

It all began because it had been raining for three weeks and we had no work. We began to gather our things and made ready to leave. We had been with that farmer in Minnesota waiting for the rain to stop but it never did. Then he came and told us that the best thing for us to do was to leave his shacks because, after all, the beets had begin to rot away already. We understood, my father and I, that he was in fact afraid of us. He was afraid that we would begin to steal from him or perhaps that one of us would get sick, and then he would have to take the responsibility because we had no money. We told him we had no money, neither did we have anything to eat and no way of making it all the way back to Texas. We had enough money, perhaps, to buy gasoline to get as far south as Oklahoma. He just told us that he was very sorry, but he wanted us to leave. So we began to pick up our things. We were leaving when he softened up somewhat and gave us two tents, full of spiderwebs, that he had in the loft in one of his barns. He also gave us a lamp and some kerosene. He told my dad that, if we went by way of Crystal Lake in northern Iowa, perhaps we would find work among the farmers and perhaps it had not been raining there so much and the beets had not rotted away. And we left.

In my father's eyes and in my mother's eyes, I saw something original and pure that I had never seen before. It was a sad type of love, it seemed. We barely talked as we went riding over the gravel roads. The rain seemed to talk for us. A few miles before reaching Crystal Lake, we began to get remorseful. The rain that continued to fall kept on telling us monotonously that we would surely not find work there. And so it was. At every farm that we came to, the farmers would only shake their heads from inside the house. They would not even open the door to tell us there was no work. It was when they shook their heads in this way that I began to feel that I was not part of my father and mother. The only thing in my mind that existed was the following farm.

The first day we were in the little town of Crystal Lake everything went bad. Going through a puddle, the car's wiring got wet and my father drained the battery trying to get the car started. Finally, a garage did us the favor of recharging the battery. We asked for work in various parts of the little town, but then they got the police after us. My father explained that we were only looking for work, but the policeman told us that he did not want any gypsies in town and told us to leave. The money was almost all gone, but we had to leave. We left at twilight and we stopped the car some three miles from town and there we saw the night fall.

The rain would come and go. Seated in the car near the ditch, we spoke little. We were tired. We were hungry. We were alone. We sensed that we were totally alone. In my father's eyes and in my mother's eyes, I saw something original. That day we had hardly eaten anything in order to have money left for the following day. My father looked sadder, weakened. He believed we would find no work, and we stayed seated in the car waiting for the following day. Almost no cars passed by on that gravel road during the night. At dawn I awoke and everybody was asleep, and I could see their bodies and their faces. I could see the bodies of my mother and my father and my brothers and sisters, and they were silent. They were faces and bodies made of wax. They reminded me of my grandfather's face the day we buried him. But I didn't get as afraid as that day when I found him inside the truck, dead. I guess it was because I knew they were not dead and that they were alive. Finally, the day came completely.

That day we looked for work all day, and we didn't find any work. We slept at the edge of the ditch and again I awoke in the early morning hours. Again I saw my people asleep. And that morning I felt somewhat afraid, not because they looked as if they were dead, but because I began to feel again that I no longer belonged to them.

The following day we looked for work all day again, and nothing. We slept at the edge of the ditch. Again I awoke in the morning, and again I saw my people asleep. But that morning, the third one, I felt like leaving them because I truly felt that I was no longer a part of them.

On that day, by noon, the rain stopped and the sun

came out and we were filled with hope. Two hours later we had found a farmer who had some beets that, according to him, probably had not been spoiled by the rain. But he had no houses or anything to live in. He showed us the acres of beets which were still under water, and he told us that, if we cared to wait until the water went down to see if the beets had not rotted, and if they had not, he would pay us a large bonus per acre that we helped him cultivate. But he didn't have any houses, he told us. We told him we had some tents with us, and, if he would let us, we would set them up in his yard. But he didn't want that. We noticed that he was afraid of us. The only thing that we wanted was to be near the drinking water, which was necessary, and also we were so tired of sleeping seated in the car, and, of course, we wanted to be under the light that he had in his yard. But he did not want us, and he told us, if we wanted to work there, we had to put our tents at the foot of the field and wait there for the water to go down. And so we placed our tents at the foot of the field and we began to wait. At nightfall we lit up the lamp in one of the tents, and then we decided for all of us to sleep in one tent only. I remember that we all felt so comfortable being able to stretch our legs, our arms, and falling asleep was easy. The thing that I remember so clearly that night was what awakened me. I felt what I thought was the hand of one of my little brothers, and then I heard my own screaming. I pulled his hand away, and, when I awoke, I found myself holding a salamander. Then I screamed and I saw that we were all covered with salamanders that had come out from the flooded fields. And all of us continued screaming and throwing salamanders off our bodies. With the light of the lamp, we began to kill them. At first we felt nauseated because, when we stepped on them, they would ooze milk. It seemed they were invading us, that they were invading the tent as if they wanted to reclaim the foot of the field. I don't know why we killed so many salamanders that night. The easiest thing to do would have been to climb quickly into our car. Now that I remember, I think that we also felt the desire to recover and to reclaim the foot of the field. I do remember that we began to look for more salamanders to kill. We wanted to find more to kill more. I remember that I liked to take the lamp, to seek them out, to kill them very slowly. It may be that I was angry at them for having frightened me. Then I began to feel that I was becoming part of my father and my mother and my brothers and sisters again.

What I remember most about that night was the darkness, the mud and the slime of the salamanders, and how they would get when I tried to squeeze the life out of them. What I have with me still is what I saw and felt when I killed the last one, and I guess that is why I remember the night of the salamanders. I caught one and examined it very carefully under the lamp. Then I looked at its eyes for a long time before I killed it. What I saw and what I felt is something I still have with me, something that is very pure—original death.

Seventeen Syllables

■ ■ ■

Hisaye Yamamoto

The first Rosie knew that her mother had taken to writing poems was one evening when she finished one and read it aloud for her daughter's approval. It was about cats, and Rosie pretended to understand it thoroughly and appreciate it no end, partly because she hesitated to disillusion her mother about the quantity and quality of Japanese she had learned in all the years now that she had been going to Japanese school every Saturday (and Wednesday, too, in the summer). Even so, her mother must have been skeptical about the depth of Rosie's understanding, because she explained afterwards about the kind of poem she was trying to write.

See, Rosie, she said, it was a *haiku*, a poem in which she must pack all her meaning into seventeen syllables only, which were divided into three lines of five, seven, and five syllables. In the one she had just read, she had tried to capture the charm of a kitten, as well as comment on the superstition that owning a cat of three colors meant good luck.

"Yes, yes, I understand. How utterly lovely," Rosie said, and her mother, either satisfied or seeing through the deception and resigned, went back to composing.

The truth was that Rosie was lazy; English lay ready on the tongue but Japanese had to be searched for and examined, and even then put forth tentatively (probably to meet with laughter). It was so much easier to say yes, yes, even when one meant no, no. Besides, this was what was in her mind to say: I was looking through one of your magazines from Japan last night, Mother, and towards the back I found some *haiku* in English that delighted me. There was one that made me giggle off and on until I fell asleep—

> *It is morning, and lo!*
> *I lie awake, comme il faut,*
> *sighing for some dough.*

Now, how to reach her mother, how to communicate the melancholy song? Rosie knew formal Japanese by fits and starts, her mother had even less English, no French. It was much more possible to say yes, yes.

It developed that her mother was writing the *haiku* for a daily newspaper, the *Mainichi Shimbun*, which was published in San Francisco. Los Angeles, to be sure, was closer to the farming community in which the Hayashi family lived and several Japanese vernaculars were printed there, but Rosie's parents said they preferred the tone of the northern paper. Once a week, the *Mainichi* would have a section devoted to *haiku*, and her mother became an extravagant contributor, taking for herself the blossoming pen name, Ume Hanazono.

So Rosie and her father lived for a while with two women, her mother and Ume Hanazono. Her mother (Tome Hayashi by name) kept house, cooked, washed, and, along with her husband and the Carrascos, the Mexican family hired for the harvest, did her ample share of picking tomatoes out in the sweltering fields and boxing them in tidy strata in the cool packing shed. Ume Hanazono, who came to life after the dinner dishes were done, was an earnest, muttering stranger who often neglected speaking when spoken to and stayed busy at the parlor table as late as midnight scribbling with pencil on scratch paper or carefully copying characters on good paper with her fat, pale green Parker.

The new interest had some repercussions on the household routine. Before, Rosie had been accustomed to her parents and herself taking their hot baths early and going to bed almost immediately afterwards, unless her parents challenged each other to a game of flower cards or unless company dropped in. Now if her father wanted to play cards, he had to resort to solitaire (at which he always cheated fearlessly), and if a group of friends came over, it was bound to contain someone who was also writing *haiku*, and the small assemblage would be split in two, her father entertaining the non-literary members and her mother comparing ecstatic notes with the visiting poet.

It they went out, it was more of the same thing. But Ume Hanazono's life span, even for a poet's, was very brief—perhaps three months at most.

One night they went over to see the Hayano family in the neighboring town to the west, an adventure both painful and attractive to Rosie. It was attractive because there were four Hayano girls, all lovely and each one named after a season of the year (Haru, Natsu, Aki, Fuyu), painful because something had been wrong with Mrs. Hayano ever since the birth of her first child. Rosie would sometimes watch Mrs. Hayano, reputed to have been the belle of her native village, making her way about a room, stooped, slowly shuffling, violently trembling (*always* trembling), and she would be reminded that this woman, in this same condition, had carried and given issue to three babies. She would look wonderingly at Mr. Hayano, handsome, tall, and strong, and she would look at her four pretty friends. But it was not a matter she could come to any decision about.

On this visit, however, Mrs. Hayano sat all evening in the rocker, as motionless and unobtrusive as it was possible for her to be, and Rosie found the greater part of the evening practically anesthetic. Too, Rosie spent most of it in the girls' room, because Haru, the garrulous one, said almost as soon as the bows and other greetings were over, "Oh, you must see my new coat!"

It was a pale plaid of gray, sand, and blue, with an enormous collar, and Rosie, seeing nothing special in it, said, "Gee, how nice."

"Nice?" said Haru, indignantly. "Is that all you can say about it? It's gorgeous! And so cheap, too. Only seventeen-ninety-eight, because it was a sale. The saleslady said it was twenty-five dollars regular."

"Gee," said Rosie. Natsu, who never said much and when she said anything said it shyly, fingered the coat covetously and Haru pulled it away.

"Mine," she said, putting it on. She minced in the aisle between the two large beds and smiled happily. "Let's see how your mother likes it."

She broke into the front room and the adult conversation and went to stand in front of Rosie's mother, while the rest watched from the door. Rosie's mother was properly envious. "May I inherit it when you're through with it?"

Haru, pleased, giggled and said yes, she could, but

Natsu reminded gravely from the door, "You promised me, Haru."

Everyone laughed but Natsu, who shamefacedly retreated into the bedroom. Haru came in laughing, taking off the coat. "We were only kidding, Natsu," she said. "Here, you try it on now."

After Natsu buttoned herself into the coat, inspected herself solemnly in the bureau mirror, and reluctantly shed it, Rosie, Aki, and Fuyu got their turns, and Fuyu, who was eight, drowned in it while her sisters and Rosie doubled up in amusement. They all went into the front room later, because Haru's mother quaveringly called to her to fix the tea and rice cakes and open a can of sliced peaches for everybody. Rosie noticed that her mother and Mr. Hayano were talking together at the little table—they were discussing a *haiku* that Mr. Hayano was planning to send to the *Mainichi*, while her father was sitting at one end of the sofa looking through a copy of *Life*, the new picture magazine. Occasionally, her father would comment on a photograph, holding it toward Mrs. Hayano and speaking to her as he always did—loudly, as though he thought someone such as she must surely be at least a trifle deaf also.

The five girls had their refreshments at the kitchen table, and it was while Rosie was showing the sisters her trick of swallowing peach slices without chewing (she chased each slippery crescent down with a swig of tea) that her father brought his empty teacup and untouched saucer to the sink and said, "Come on, Rosie, we're going home now."

"Already?" asked Rosie.

"Work tomorrow," he said.

He sounded irritated, and Rosie, puzzled, gulped one

last yellow slice and stood up to go, while the sisters began protesting, as was their wont.

"We have to get up at five-thirty," he told them, going into the front room quickly, so that they did not have their usual chance to hang onto his hands and plead for an extension of time.

Rosie, following, saw that her mother and Mr. Hayano were sipping tea and still talking together, while Mrs. Hayano concentrated, quivering, on raising the handleless Japanese cup to her lips with both her hands and lowering it back to her lap. Her father, saying nothing, went out the door, onto the bright porch, and down the steps. Her mother looked up and asked, "Where is he going?"

"Where is he going?" Rosie said. "He said we were going home now."

"Going home?" Her mother looked with embarrassment at Mr. Hayano and his absorbed wife and then forced a smile. "He must be tired," she said.

Haru was not giving up yet. "May Rosie stay overnight?" she asked, and Natsu, Aki, and Fuyu came to reinforce their sister's plea by helping her make a circle around Rosie's mother. Rosie, for once having no desire to stay, was relieved when her mother, apologizing to the perturbed Mr. and Mrs. Hayano for her father's abruptness at the same time, managed to shake her head no at the quartet, kindly but adamant, so that they broke their circle and let her go.

Rosie's father looked ahead into the windshield as the two joined him. "I'm sorry," her mother said. "You must be tired." Her father, stepping on the starter, said nothing. "You know how I get when it's *haiku*," she continued, "I forget what time it is." He only grunted.

As they rode homeward silently, Rosie, sitting between, felt a rush of hate for both—for her mother for begging, for her father for denying her mother. I wish this old Ford would crash, right now, she thought, then immediately, no, no, I wish my father would laugh, but it was too late: already the vision had passed through her mind of the green pickup crumpled in the dark against one of the mighty eucalyptus trees they were just riding past, of the three contorted, bleeding bodies, one of them hers.

Rosie ran between two patches of tomatoes, her heart working more rambunctiously than she had ever known it to. How lucky it was that Aunt Taka and Uncle Gimpachi had come tonight, though, how very lucky. Otherwise she might now have really kept her half-promise to meet Jesus Carrasco. Jesus was going to be a senior in September at the same school she went to, and his parents were the ones helping with the tomatoes this year. She and Jesus, who hardly remembered seeing each other at Cleveland High where there were so many other people and two whole grades between them, had become great friends this summer—he always had a joke for her when he periodically drove the loaded pickup up from the fields to the shed where she was usually sorting while her mother and father did the packing, and they laughed a great deal together over infinitesimal repartee during the afternoon break for chilled watermelon or ice cream in the shade of the shed.

What she enjoyed most was racing him to see which could finish picking a double row first. He, who could work faster, would tease her by slowing down until she thought she would surely pass him this time, then speeding up furiously to leave her several sprawling vines behind. Once he had made her screech hideously by crossing over, while her back was turned, to place atop the tomatoes in her green-stained bucket a truly monstrous, pale green worm (it had looked more like an infant snake). And it was when they had finished a contest this morning, in the lugs at the end of his row and he had returned the accusation (with justice), that he had startlingly brought up the matter of their possibly meeting outside the range of both their parents' dubious eyes.

"What for?" she had asked.

"I've got a secret I want to tell you," he said.

"Tell me now," she demanded.

"It won't be ready till tonight," he said.

She laughed. "Tell me tomorrow then."

"It'll be gone tomorrow," he threatened.

"Well, for seven hakes, what it is?" she had asked, more than twice, and when he had suggested that the packing shed would be an appropriate place to find out, she had cautiously answered maybe. She had not been certain she was going to keep the appointment until the arrival of mother's sister and her husband. Their coming seemed a sort of signal of permission, of grace, and she had definitely made up her mind to lie and leave as she was bowing them welcome.

So as soon as everyone appeared settled back for the evening, she announced loudly that she was going to the privy outside, "I'm going to the *benjo!*" and slipped out the door. And now that she was actually on her way, her heart pumped in such an undisciplined way that she could hear it with her ears. It's because I'm running, she told herself, slowing to a walk. The shed was up ahead, one more patch away, in the middle of the fields. Its bulk, looming in the dimness, took on a sinisterness that was funny when Rosie reminded herself that it was only a wooden frame with a canvas roof and three canvas walls that made a slapping noise on breezy days.

Jesus was sitting on the narrow plank that was the sorting platform and she went around to the other side and jumped backwards to seat herself on the rim of a packing stand. "Well, tell me," she said without greeting, thinking her voice sounded reassuringly familiar.

"I saw you coming out the door," Jesus said. "I heard you running part of the way, too."

"Uh-huh," Rosie said. "Now tell me the secret."

"I was afraid you wouldn't come," he said.

Rosie delved around on the chicken-wire bottom of the stall for number two tomatoes, ripe, which she was sitting beside, and came up with a left-over that felt edible. She bit into it and began sucking out the pulp and seeds. "I'm here," she pointed out.

"Rosie, are you sorry you came?"

"Sorry? What for?" she said. "You said you were going to tell me something."

"I will, I will," Jesus said, but his voice contained disappointment, and Rosie fleetingly felt the older of the two, realizing a brand-new power which vanished without category under her recognition.

"I have to go back in a minute," she said. " My aunt and uncle are here from Wintersburg. I told them I was going to the privy."

Jesus laughed. "You funny thing," he said. "You slay me!"

"Just because you have a bathroom *inside*," Rosie said. "Come on, tell me."

Chuckling, Jesus came around to lean on the stand facing her. They still could not see each other very clearly, but Rosie noticed that Jesus became very sober again as he took the hollow tomato from her and dropped it back into the stall. When he took hold of her empty hand, she could find no words to protest; her vocabulary had become distressingly constricted and she thought desperately that all that remained intact now was yes and no and oh, and even these few sounds would not easily out. Thus, kissed by Jesus, Rosie fell for the first time entirely victim to a helplessness delectable beyond speech. But the terrible, beautiful sensation lasted no more than a second, and the reality of Jesus' lips and tongue and teeth and hands made her pull away with such strength that she nearly tumbled.

Rosie stopped running as she approached the lights from the windows of home. How long since she had left? She could not guess, but gasping yet, she went to the privy in back and locked herself in. Her own breathing deafened her in the dark, close space, and she sat and waited until she could hear at last the nightly calling of the frogs and crickets. Even then, all she could think to say was oh, my, and the pressure of Jesus' face against her face would not leave.

No one missed her in the parlor, however, and Rosie walked in and through quickly, announcing that she was next going to take a bath. "Your father's in the bathhouse," her mother said, and Rosie, in her room, recalled that she had not seen him when she entered. There had been only Aunt Taka and Uncle Gimpachi with her mother at the table, drinking tea. She got her robe and straw sandals and crossed the parlor again to go outside. Her mother was telling them about the *haiku* competition in the *Mainichi* and the poem she had entered.

Rosie met her father coming out of the bathhouse. "Are you through, Father?" she asked. "I was going to ask you to scrub my back."

"Scrub your own back," he said shortly, going toward the main house.

"What have I done now?" she yelled after him. She suddenly felt like doing a lot of yelling. But he did not answer, and she went into the bathhouse. Turning on the dangling light, she removed her denims and T-shirt and threw them in the big carton for dirty clothes standing next to the washing machine. Her other things she took with her into the bath compartment to wash after her bath. After she had scooped a basin of hot water from the square wooden tub, she sat on the gray cement of the floor and soaped herself at exaggerated leisure, singing "Red Sails in the Sunset" at the top of her voice and using da-da-da where she suspected her words. Then, standing up, still singing, for she was possessed by the notion that any attempt now to analyze would result in spoilage and she believed that the larger her volume the less she would be able to hear herself think, she obtained more hot water and poured it on until she was free of lather. Only then did she allow herself to step into the steaming vat, one leg first, then the remainder of her body inch by inch until the water no longer stung and she could move around at will.

She took a long time soaking, afterwards remembering to go around outside to stoke the embers of the tin-lined fireplace beneath the tub and to throw on a few more sticks so that the water might keep its heat for her mother, and when she finally returned to the parlor, she found her mother still talking *haiku* with her aunt and uncle, the three of them on another round of tea. Her father was nowhere in sight.

At Japanese school the next day (Wednesday, it was), Rosie was grave and giddy by turns. Preoccupied at her desk in the row for students on Book Eight, she made up for it at recess by performing wild mimicry for the benefit of her friend Chizuko. She held her nose and whined a witticism or two in what she considered was the manner of Fred Allen; she assumed intoxication and a British accent to go over the climax of the Rudy Vallee recording of the pub conversation about William Ewart Gladstone; she was the child Shirley Temple piping, "On the Good Ship Lollipop"; she was the gentleman soprano of the Four Ink Spots trilling, "If I Didn't Care." And she felt reasonably satisfied when Chizuko wept and gasped, "Oh, Rosie, you ought to be in the movies!"

Her father came after her at noon, bringing her sandwiches of minced ham and two nectarines to eat while she rode, so that she could pitch right into the sorting when they got home. The lugs were piling up, he said, and the ripe tomatoes in them would probably have to be taken to the cannery tomorrow if they were not ready for the produce haulers tonight. "This heat's not doing them any good. And we've got no time for a break today."

It *was* hot, probably the hottest day of the year, and

Rosie's blouse stuck damply to her back even under the protection of the canvas. But she worked as efficiently as a flawless machine and kept the stalls heaped, with one part of her mind listening in to the parental mumuring about the heat and the tomatoes and with another part planning the exact words she would say to Jesus when he drove up with the first load of the afternoon. But when at last she saw that the pickup was coming, her hands went berserk and the tomatoes started falling in the wrong stalls, and her father said, "Hey, hey! Rosie, watch what you're doing!"

"Well, I have to go to the *benjo*," she said, hiding panic.

"Go in the weeds over there," he said, only half-joking.

"Oh, Father!" she protested.

"Oh, go on home," her mother said. "We'll make out for a while."

In the privy Rosie peered through a knothole toward the fields, watching as much as she could of Jesus. Happily she thought she saw him look in the direction of the house from time to time before he finished unloading and went back toward the patch where his mother and father worked. As she was heading for the shed, a very presentable black car purred up the dirt driveway to the house and its driver motioned to her. Was this the Hayashi home, he wanted to know. She nodded. Was she a Hayashi? Yes, she said, thinking that he was a good-looking man. He got out of the car with a huge, flat package and she saw that he warmly wore a business suit. " I have something here for your mother then," he said, in a more elegant Japanese than she was used to.

She told him where her mother was and he came

along with her, patting his face with an immaculate white handkerchief and saying something about the coolness of San Francisco. To her surprised mother and father, he bowed and introduced himself as, among other things, the *haiku* editor of the *Mainichi Shimbun*, saying that since he had been coming as far as Los Angeles anyway, he had decided to bring her the first prize she had won in the recent contest.

"First prize?" her mother echoed, believing and not believing, pleased and overwhelmed. Handed the package with a bow, she bobbed her head up and down numerous times to express her utter gratitude.

"It is nothing much," he added, "but I hope it will serve as a token of our great appreciation for your contributions and out great admiration of your considerable talent."

"I am not worthy," she said, falling easily into his style. "It is I who should make some sign of my humble thanks for being permitted to contribute."

"No, no, to the contrary," he said, bowing again.

But Rosie's mother insisted, and then saying that she knew she was being unorthodox, she asked if she might open the package because her curiosity was so great. Certainly she might. In fact, he would like her reaction to it, for personally, it was one of his favorite Hiroshiges.

Rosie thought it was a pleasant picture, which looked to have been sketched with delicate quickness. There were pink clouds, containing some graceful calligraphy, and a sea that was a pale blue except at the edges, containing four sampans with indications of people in them. Pines edged the water and on the far-off beach there was a cluster of thatched huts towered over by pine-dotted mountains of gray and blue. The frame was scalloped and gilt.

After Rosie's mother pronounced it without peer and somewhat prodded her father into nodding agreement, she said Mr. Kuroda must at least have a cup of tea after coming all this way, and although Mr. Kuroda did not want to impose, he soon agreed that a cup of tea would be refreshing and went along with her to the house, carrying the picture for her.

"Ha, your mother's crazy!" Rosie's father said, and Rosie laughed uneasily as she resumed judgment on the tomatoes. She had emptied six lugs when he broke into an imaginary conversation with Jesus to tell her to go remind her mother of the tomatoes, and she went slowly.

Mr. Kuroda was in his shirtsleeves expounding some *haiku* theory as he munched a rice cake, and her mother was rapt. Abashed in the great man's presence, Rosie stood next to her mother's chair until her mother looked up inquiringly, and then she started to whisper the message, but her mother pushed her gently away and reproached, "You are not being very polite to our guest."

"Father says the tomatoes . . . " Rosie said aloud, smiling foolishly.

"Tell him I shall only be a minute," her mother said, speaking the language of Mr. Kuroda.

When Rosie carried the reply to her father, he did not seem to hear and she said again, "Mother says she'll be back in a minute."

"All right, all right," he nodded, and they worked again in silence. But suddenly, her father uttered an incredible noise, exactly like the cork of a bottle pop-ping, and the next Rosie knew, he was stalking angrily toward the house, almost running in fact, and she chased after him crying, "Father! Father! What are you going to do?"

He stopped long enough to order her back to the shed. "Never mind!" he shouted. "Get on with the sorting!"

And from the place in the fields where she stood, frightened and vacillating, Rosie saw her father enter the house. Soon Mr. Kuroda came out alone, putting on his coat. Mr. Kuroda got into his car and backed out down the driveway onto the highway. Next her father emerged, also alone, something in his arms (it was the picture, she realized), and, going over to the bathhouse woodpile, he threw the picture on the ground and picked up the axe. Smashing the picture, glass and all (she heard the explosion faintly), he reached over for the kerosene that was used to encourage the bath fire and poured it over the wreckage. I am dreaming, Rosie said to herself, I am dreaming, but her father, having made sure that his act of cremation was irrevocable, was even then returning to the fields.

Rosie ran past him and toward the house. What had become of her mother? She burst into the parlor and found her mother at the back window watching the dying fire. They watched together until there remained only a feeble smoke under the blazing sun. Her mother was very calm.

"Do you know why I married your father?" she said without turning.

"No," said Rosie. It was the most frightening question she had ever been called upon to answer. Don't tell me now, she wanted to say, tell me tomorrow, tell me next week, don't tell me today. But she knew she would be told now, that the telling would combine with the other violence of the hot afternoon to level her life, her world to the very ground.

It was like a story out of the magazines illustrated in sepia, which she had consumed so greedily for a period until the information had somehow reached her that those wretchedly unhappy autobiographies, offered to her as the testimonials of living men and women, were largely inventions: Her mother, at nineteen, had come to America and married her father as an alternative to suicide.

At eighteen she had been in love with the first son of one of the well-to-do families in her village. The two had met whenever and wherever they could, secretly, because it would not have done for his family to see him favor her—her father had no money; he was a drunkard and a gambler besides. She had learned she was with child; an excellent match had already been arranged for her lover. Despised by her family, she had given premature birth to a stillborn son, who would be seventeen now. Her family did not turn her out, but she could no longer project herself in any direction without refreshing in them the memory of her indiscretion. She wrote to Aunt Taka, her favorite sister in America, threatening to kill herself if Aunt Taka would not send for her. Aunt Taka hastily arranged a young man of whom she knew, but lately arrived from Japan, a young man of simple mind, it was said, but of kindly heart. The young man was never told why his unseen betrothed was so eager to hasten the day of meeting.

The story was told perfectly, with neither groping for words nor untoward passion. It was as though her mother had memorized it by heart, reciting it to herself so many times over that its nagging vileness had long since gone.

"I had a brother then?" Rosie asked, for this was what seemed to matter now; she would think about the other later, she assured herself, pushing back the illumination which threatened all that darkness that had hitherto been merely mysterious or even glamorous. "A half-brother?"

"Yes."

"I would have liked a brother," she said.

Suddenly, her mother knelt on the floor and took her by the wrists. "Rosie," she said urgently, "Promise me you will never marry!" Shocked more by the request than the revelation, Rosie started at her mother's face. Jesus, Jesus, she called silently, not certain whether she was invoking the help of the son of the Carrascos or of God, until there returned sweetly the memory of Jesus' hand, how it had touched her and where. Still her mother waited for an answer, holding her wrists so tightly that her hands were going numb. She tried to pull free. Promise, her mother whispered fiercely, promise. Yes, yes, I promise, Rosie said. But for an instant she turned away, and her mother, hearing the familiar glib agreement, released her. Oh, you, you, you, her eyes and twisted mouth said, you fool. Rosie, covering her face, began at last to cry, and the embrace and consoling hand came much later than she expected.

Biographical Notes on the Authors

PINCKNEY BENEDICT (b. 1964) grew up in the mountains of southern West Virginia. He was awarded the Nelson Algren Award at the age of twenty-three and is the author of two story collections—*Town Smokes* and *The Wrecking Yard*—and the novel *Dogs of God*. He teaches creative writing at Hollins University in Roanoke, Virginia.

NANCY K. BROWN (b. 1950) has never lived outside California, and her farming roots go back several generations. She currently lives in Bonny Doon, a small ranch in the Santa Cruz Mountains, with four horses, two dogs, two cats, a cockatoo, four sons, and her husband Glen, a first-generation ranch hand. "Burn Pile" is the first work she has ever had published or submitted for publication.

NORA MARKS DAUENHAUER (b. 1927) first spoke only her native Tlingit but started learning English at the age of eight. She was raised in Juneau and Hoonah and on her family's fishing boat that traveled to seasonal subsistence sites around Icy Straits, Glacier Bay, and Cape Spencer. She has a B.A. in anthropology and is recognized internationally for her fieldwork, transcriptions, translations, and explications of Tlingit oral literature. Her poetry, prose, and drama have been widely published and anthologized.

TONY EARLEY (b. 1961) is a North Carolina journalist and the author of several works of fiction, including the short story collection *Here We Are in Paradise* and the highly acclaimed novel *Jim the Boy*.

ERIC L. GANSWORTH (b. 1965), an enrolled member of the Onondaga Nation, was born and raised on the Tuscarora Indian Reservation in New York. He is a painter and photographer, as well as writer, and teaches at Niagara County Community College. Besides numerous publications in journals and anthologies, his published works include the novel *Indian Summers* and, most recently, *Nickel Eclipse: Iroquois Moon*, a collection of poetry that includes his own paintings.

JIM HEYNEN (b. 1940) now lives in St. Paul, Minnesota, and teaches writing at St. Olaf College in Northfield, but was born and raised on a farm in northwest Iowa where he attended a one-room schoolhouse for his first eight years of school. His most recent books include *The Boys' House: New and Selected Stories, Standing Naked: New and Selected Poems,* and two novels for young adults—*Cosmos Coyote and William the Nice* and *Being Youngest.* Earlier collections of short stories include *The One-Room Schoolhouse.*

LEWIS NORDAN (b. 1939) was born in Forest, Mississippi, and raised by Southern storytellers in Itta Bena, Mississippi. He is the author of several works of fiction, including the novel *The Sharpshooter Blues,* which was a 1995 American Library Association Notable Book, and the short story collection *Sugar Among the Freaks.*

TOMÁS RIVERA (1935-1984) was a native of Crystal City, Texas. The son of Mexican immigrants, he and his family were seasonal farm workers who followed the harvests into the Midwest. Rivera earned a doctorate in Romance languages and literature and is best known for his novel *. . . y no se lo tago' la tierra (And the Earth Did Not Devour Him).*

REBECCA RULE (b. 1954) was born in New Hampshire and has never lived outside the state. She is the author of the short story collection *The Best Revenge* and co-author of the writing how-to books *Creating the Story: Guides for Writers* and, most recently, *True Stories: Guides for Writing from your Life.* She also has produced two humorous audiotapes: "Perley Gets a Dump Sticker and Other Harrowing Tales" and "Fishing with George."

WALLACE STEGNER (1909-1993) was born in Iowa and went on to become a distinguished writer, historian, and teacher. His short stories won three O. Henry Prizes, his novels a National Book Award (*The Spectator Bird*), the Pulitzer Prize (*Angle of Repose*), and the Commonwealth Gold Medal for *All The Little Things.* He is the author of sixteen books of fiction and eleven books of nonfiction. He taught at Harvard, the University of Iowa, the University of Utah, and for many years at Stanford, where the Stegner Fellowship program is named in his honor.

KATHLEEN TYAU (b. 1947), of Native Hawaiian-Chinese descent, grew up on the island of Oahu before going to college at Lewis and Clark in Portland, Oregon. She is the author of two novels set in Hawaii, *A Little Too Much Is Enough* and *Makai.* Her awards include the Pacific Northwest Booksellers Award and a National Endowment for the Arts

Fellowship. She currently lives with her husband on a tree farm in northwest Oregon where she writes and plays bluegrass guitar and mandolin.

ALMA VILLANUEVA (b. 1944) was born in Lompoc, California, and is the author of a novel, *The Ultraviolet Sky*, and several collections of poetry, including *Bloodroot* and the long narrative poem *Mother, May I?* She was first-place winner in the Third Chicano Literary Prize from the University of California at Irvine. She is the author of several children's stories and is a frequent contributor to high school textbooks.

JON VOLKMER (b. 1956) is a prize-winning fiction writer, a regular reviewer for *The Philadelphia Inquirer,* and the Director of Creative Writing at Ursinus College in Collegeville, Pennsylvania. He has also published poetry, personal essays, travel writing, and feature pieces. His book, *The Fiction Workshop Companion*, is designed for use in high school and college classes.

ALICE WALKER (b. 1944) was born in Eaton, Georgia, and is the author of many volumes of essays, poems, short stories, and novels, including *The Color Purple*, which won the Pulitzer Prize in 1983, and *In Love and Trouble: Stories of Black Women*.

VICKY WICKS (b. 1953) has several published short stories and is a graduate of the master's program in English at the University of South Dakota. She has been a journalist and now works in the Brown County Victim Assistance program in Aberdeen, South Dakota. She has completed a novel that is now in search of a publisher.

HISAYE YAMAMOTO (b. 1921) was one of the first Japanese American authors to get national attention after the Second World War. She was born in Redondo, California, to first-generation immigrants. In her early twenties she was sent to the Poston Relocation Center in Arizona and was interned with other Japanese Americans for three years. Many of her stories have appeared in anthologies, including *Best American Short Stories, 1952.* Her first collection of short stories was *Seventeen Syllables and Other Stories*, published in 1988.